Emily found her patient in an agitated state

The usually troublesome Lucillia cried, ''Emily, you won't go away, will you? Sebastian says you will, if I can't stop behaving like a spoiled baby. He's not often angry, you know, but he was then. He said you were a treasure and he'd never find your equal, even if he searched the world over.''

Emily felt a glow of excitement, although she didn't know why.... It was immediately doused as Lucillia went on, ''He says you're the best nurse he has had to deal with for years.''

''How very kind,'' said Emily in a flat, disappointed voice.

What on earth had possessed her—even momentarily—to suppose that Sebastian had meant anything else?

Dear Reader:

We hope our December Harlequin Romances bring you many hours of enjoyment this holiday season.

1989 was an exciting year. We published our 3000th Harlequin Romance! And we introduced a new cover design—which we hope you like.

We're wrapping up the year with a terrific selection of satisfying stories, written by your favorite authors, as well as by some very talented newcomers we're introducing to the series. As always, we've got settings guaranteed to take you places—from the English Cotswolds, to New Zealand, to Holland, to some hometown settings in the United States.

So when you need a break from the hustle and bustle of preparing for the holidays, sit back and relax with our heartwarming stories. Stories with laughter...a few tears...and lots of heart.

And later, when you get a chance, drop us a line with your thoughts and ideas about how we can try to make your enjoyment of Harlequin Romances even better in the years to come.

From our house to yours, Happy Holidays! And may this special season bring you a lasting gift of joy and happiness.

The Editors
Harlequin Romance
225 Duncan Mill Road
Don Mills, Ontario, Canada
M3B 3K9

THE FATEFUL BARGAIN
Betty Neels

Harlequin Books

TORONTO • NEW YORK • LONDON
AMSTERDAM • PARIS • SYDNEY • HAMBURG
STOCKHOLM • ATHENS • TOKYO • MILAN

Original hardcover edition published in 1989
by Mills & Boon Limited

ISBN 0-373-03024-X

Harlequin Romance first edition December 1989

CHAPTER ONE

SUMMER LANE wasn't living up to its name; for one thing it was mid-October and the rain, being lashed down by a nasty chilly wind, was even chillier; moreover it was barely eight o'clock in the morning and gloomy. At that early time of day there were few people about; a milkman whistling defiantly as he dumped down milk bottles, a handful of people scurrying along towards the nearest Tube station and a solitary girl walking away from it, head bowed against the weather, clutching a plastic bag. The street lined with shabby old houses, let out in rooms or flats, was so familiar to her that she didn't bother to look up as it turned a sharp corner, which was why she ran full tilt into someone coming the other way.

The plastic bag, already wet, split and spilled its contents over the pavement, and the girl skidded to a halt which almost took her feet from under her, to be hauled upright by a powerful arm.

'You should look where you are going,' the owner of the arm observed irritably, a remark the girl took instant exception to; she was dog-tired after night duty and in no mood to bandy words with someone who sounded as cross as she felt.

All the same, she said in a reasonable voice, 'Well, that goes for both of us, doesn't it?' and looked up at the man towering over her. He wasn't only tall, he was large as well and remarkably good-looking, and when he smiled suddenly, she smiled back.

He let go of her then and bent to pick up the contents of the plastic bag—knitting, the wool already very wet, a rather battered manual of nursing, two apples and a notebook. He collected them, gave her the book and the knitting and said with rather impatient kindness, 'Do you live close by? Suppose I carry these odds and ends as far as your door?'

'Thank you, but I live down that street...' she indicated a narrow side street a few yards further on. 'I can stuff everything in my pockets.'

He took no notice of that but turned and started walking briskly towards the street that she had pointed out.

'A nurse?' he wanted to know.

The girl trotted beside him. 'Yes, on night duty at Pearson's. I'm not trained yet, I'm in my second year, almost at the end of it.'

She stopped before one of the elderly terraced houses, its gate wedged open, its tiny strip of garden a mass of soggy weeds. 'This is where I live.' She held her arms out for the things he had been carrying.

He didn't give them to her at first but stood looking at her. She wasn't much to look at: small, inclined to plumpness, with a nice little face redeemed from plainness by a pair of fine grey eyes. Her hair under an unfashionable woolly cap was pale brown and very wet. Her coat had seen better days, but it was well cut and her shoes and gloves, as shabby as the coat, were good. He smiled again. 'When do you go on day duty again?' he asked.

'Oh, in another week or so; it will seem very strange after two months. I like night duty, though; there aren't so many people around.'

'People?' He asked the question casually, concealing his impatience to be gone.

'Well, doctors and surgeons and Ward Sisters.' She went rather pink. 'They're a bit frightening, you know. Staff Nurse was telling me that there's a visiting honorary—a surgeon—he's Dutch and everyone is crazy about him. Because he's foreign, I suppose; I do hope I don't go on to the Orthopaedic side.'

'You have no wish to meet this foreigner?'

'No, oh, no. There was a French surgeon in the summer; he shouted at me and asked me to be quick, and I dropped a tray of instruments. I dare say that's why I'm on night duty longer than usual.' She put out a tongue to lick away a trickle of rain running down one cheek. She said breathlessly, 'I'm sorry, I'm keeping you in the rain. Thank you very much. I hope you won't be late for your work.'

She held out her arms for the apples and the notebook, said a hasty goodbye and whisked up the narrow path and in through the shabby front door. As she climbed the stairs she thought vexedly that she had talked too much; probably the man had been bored to death, and what had possessed her to chatter like that? It was quite unlike her. She was universally known at Pearson's Hospital as a quiet girl, friendly enough but shy and studious, reliably calm and collected about her work and guaranteed to give a helping hand without grumbling.

She opened her door, to be greeted by a rotund tabby cat with a slightly battered look, obviously delighted to see her.

It was nice to be in her room again after a busy night. It was small, but its windows, cheerfully curtained, overlooked the narrow back garden and, bare as it was, it was green. There wasn't much in the room: a divan bed, a small easy chair, a table by the window and a small sink and even smaller cooking stove in one corner, but it was her own just so long as she paid Mrs Winter the rent. Of course, a room in the Nurses' Home would have been more comfortable, but then she wouldn't have been able to keep Podge, and she had found him, hungry to the point of starving, several months ago, crouching in an empty doorway, and she had no intention of abandoning him to further misery. Indeed, he saved her from loneliness and was perfectly content to live with her in her cramped room, carried downstairs to the back garden when needful while Mrs Winter turned a blind eye. That lady didn't approve of pets in her house, but Emily had treated a nasty boil for her and moreover cleaned and bandaged a cut finger for one of her numerous grandchildren.

Mrs Winter came to the top of the basement stairs where she lived as Podge was borne in from the garden. ''Ere's a letter for yer,' she announced. 'Miss Emily Grenfell, it says—yer pa, I've no doubt.'

Emily took the letter and tucked it into her pocket. Having no letter box of her own, she depended on Mrs Winter to take in any post she might get. 'Yes, it's from my father,' she agreed cheerfully. 'What a beastly morning!'

'And me due at the 'airdresser's. If that Mrs Blake 'as 'er radio on too loud and wakes yer up, just tell me, and I'll give her the rough edge of me tongue.' Mrs Winter eyed Emily's tired face. 'Yer needs yer sleep, by the look of yer.'

There were one or two things to do in the meantime— Emily had had breakfast at the hospital, but Podge needed his; while he ate it she went down to the floor below and had a bath in the old-fashioned bathroom. The bath was in the centre of the small room so that getting in and out was awkward and the geyser made sinister rumbling noises and smelled of gas, but the water was hot. She made a cup of tea before she got into bed and set the alarm for four o'clock; she would need to do some shopping before she had tea and went back on duty. Podge got on to the bed with her; his warm weight was cosy on her feet as she read her father's letter.

She folded it carefully when she had finished it, put it back into its envelope, and lay thinking about its contents.

The letter was cheerful, amusing and totally free from grumbles, something which was a constant source of surprise to her; arthritis had crippled her father for the last two years, so that he was confined to a wheelchair for the greater part of the day, hobbling around his house with two sticks so that he could get his meals, helped by a woman from the village who came in for an hour or so each day. He had been waiting for a year or more to have a prosthesis, first in one hip, then in the other, and it would be another year before his turn would come. He and Emily had discussed it together and he had agreed, reluctantly, that she should continue her training. She had known then what she would do, although she had said nothing to him, and she had set about putting her plan into action without more ado. It meant leaving the comparative comfort of the Nurses' Home with its mod cons and taking a room in Summer Lane; its rent low enough to enable her to save every penny of her salary which she could spare.

She knew to a penny how much it would cost for the operation to be done privately, a considerable sum, but if she could somehow manage to get him into Pearson's... it would have to be one hip until she could save for the second, but once she was qualified she would earn more money, and in the meantime her father would be able to leave his wheelchair, even return to work. But not to his former job as bookkeeper in the large printing firm in the neighbouring town; he had been retired from there with a small pension, enough to live on but not enough to save.

Podge edged his way up the bed to lie on her chest and stare into her face, and Emily put out a hand to stroke him. Even if she were able to do so, she wouldn't go back to the Nurses' Home without him. Later, when her father was able to get about again and she was getting more money, the pair of them would move to a better neighbourhood and she would go home at least twice a month. Podge started to purr, a deep-chested rumble which soothed her busy brain into a quiet which soon deepened into sleep.

It was still raining when she got up. She attended to Podge's needs, had a cup of tea, tidied her room and went out to the grocer's on the corner of the street, where she did her frugal buying and went back home again to eat her supper of baked beans on toast and more tea.

The solid bulk of Pearson's Hospital loomed over her as she left the Underground, its windows lighted, and as she entered a side door, greeting her with a variety of sounds she had come to recognise and ignore. She left her outdoor things in the cloakroom, picked up the plastic bag holding her knitting and study books, and went unhurriedly up two flights of stairs. She was in good time, but then she always was, there was nothing to hinder her; no boyfriend to keep her lingering until the last minute, no visit to a West End cinema to see the latest film, no mother up for the day to shop, nobody to see off home again... Emily didn't allow herself any self-pity and indeed she felt none; she was doing something she had made up her mind to do, and do it she would, without fuss. She was only twenty-three, and in less than a year her father could have his first operation and she would be qualified. Beyond that she resolutely refused to think, although right at the back of her mind was the shadowy hope that one day someone might fall in love with her and marry her.

As she climbed the last flight she thought fleetingly of the man who had bumped into her. It was to be hoped that he hadn't been late for his work. She frowned. He hadn't been the usual type she saw on the streets at that early hour of the morning, he had been well dressed and had had the air of someone unworried by clocking-in machines. In a bank, she guessed vaguely, or perhaps a solicitor.

He was in fact walking unhurriedly along the corridor leading from the Orthopaedic theatre to Sister's office, where, still in a white drill trousers and green smock, he sat himself down at her desk and began to write up the notes of his patient. Someone brought him a mug of coffee which he drank absentmindedly as he wrote, presently to be joined by his Registrar, Henry Parker, and his Theatre Sister, a stern-featured lady who, on hearing that there was to be a Dutch specialist in Orthopaedics for a short period, had declared herself reluctant to work for him. 'I remember,' she had confided to the main

Theatre Sister, 'what a terrible time you had with that Frenchman, and I dare say,' she added darkly, 'that a Dutchman will be even worse.' She had drawn such a deep breath that her old-fashioned corsets had creaked. 'Foreigners!' she observed.

The Dutchman, when he arrived, had addressed her in English as fluent as her own, and had treated her with a quiet courtesy which had won her over completely. Moreover, he remained calm while he operated and never left the theatre without thanking her nicely for her services.

Rather grudgingly she had admitted that he was every bit as considerate as Mr Griffiths, the consultant he was standing in for until that gentleman had recovered from a severe attack of shingles. As for Mr Beck, the second orthopaedic surgeon, he was on the best of terms with him, and the housemen and nursing staff considered him to be the very acme of perfection. The nurses lucky enough to work on the orthopaedic wards or in theatre bought new lipsticks, made play with their eyelashes and had their hair done far more often than usual, going to meet him in corridors or on the stairs by deliberate accident, but they were forced to admit not one of them had struck even the smallest spark of interest in him.

Mr van Tecqx finished writing as Henry Parker joined him, and they spent a few minutes discussing his patients before he bade his Registrar goodnight and made his way through the hospital. He was at the head of the staircase when the muted sounds of its late evening activities recalled something to mind and he turned back to cross the corridor which would bring him to the medical wing. There were wide glass doors at each end of the landing. He glanced through the first of them and then walked its length to glance through the second door—Women's Medical, its occupants being settled for the night. The tall, rangy girl was scuttling down the ward in the direction of the sluice room, and going slowly from bed to bed, turning off lights, smoothing sheets and pausing to speak to the occupants, was the girl whom he had met that morning, very neat in her uniform, her hair smoothed into an unfashionable chignon under her cap, her small waist, nicely accentuating her pretty shape, encircled by its stiff white belt. As she paused under the bed lamp he could see her profile clearly; a very ordinary one with its slightly turned-up nose and wide mouth. He turned away with a shrug, wondering what quirk of fancy had made him seek her out, and went on his way down to the entrance hall, to pause at the porter's lodge and exchange goodnights with Briggs the head porter, before walking unhurriedly through the main entrance, to get into the dark grey Bentley parked outside and drive himself away.

Emily finished her round and went back to Sister's desk to con the day report and check that she had done everything necessary. Pearson's was in the process of being modernised, but the Medical Wing was to be the last to be updated, so that instead of the nurses' stations, smaller wards and day rooms with TV, and elaborate systems connecting patients with nurses, the ward she was on was long and narrow; ten beds on either side with a table in the centre and bathrooms and sluice room at the far end; in the early hours of the morning, when their energy was at its lowest ebb, leaving the desk to go to the sluice room seemed like a day's journey. All the same, the ward was a cheerful place, mainly because the Sister in charge of it was young and cheerful herself.

Emily shrouded the desk lamp with a red cloth, opened the Report Book and Kardex, and bent her neat head over them. Two barium meals for the next day, she noted; they would have to be started at a busy time of their morning too, and both ladies were bad patients. They would roll the narrow catheter round and round in their mouths instead of swallowing it, and precious minutes would be lost... She smiled at her junior nurse as she drew up a chair and sat down beside her; she liked Stella, who worked hard and didn't grumble overmuch at the endless bedpans and cups of tea which made up a major share of her night's work. They shared the work as much as possible, but inevitably Emily had to leave her to it when there was treatment of any sort.

The night went slowly and then, as it usually did, merged into a brief two hours or so of intense activity—rousing the patients with cups of tea, seeing that they went along to the bathrooms, sometimes a slow business with the elderlies who couldn't hurry and often needed an arm, doing a round with one of the Night Sisters, writing the Report, giving out medicines with her and then the final mad rush to be ready for the moment Sister came on duty. Emily went off duty at last and, careless of her appearance, ate her breakfast, exchanging sleepy gossip with the other night nurses, dragged on her coat and went out into the early morning.

The sun was shining and she breathed in the chilly air with pleasure; even if it were tainted with petrol fumes from the passing buses and the whiff from a refuse lorry, it was pleasant after a night spent in the closed ward. She made a brisk beeline for the Tube, reflecting with pleasure that pay-day was on the following morning. She would go home, she decided recklessly, taking Podge with

her in his basket. She had nights off, five of them, because she had had to cut her last lot short to fill a gap
owing to the night nurse on Men's Medical having 'flu...
She began to do sums in her head. She was still doing
them as she unlocked her door and scooped up a welcoming Podge.

'A little holiday,' she promised him as she fumbled to
fill his saucer, 'and soon I'll be on day duty and you
won't be lonely any more.'

She reflected as she got ready for bed that she would
have started her third year before the next pay-day, and
that would mean more money—another five or six
months and there would be enough saved for the first
operation. She would get hold of Day Sister and ask her
the best way to set about it. Emily closed her eyes, intending to go to sleep, but instead she found herself
thinking about the man who had almost knocked her
over. He had sounded cross and impatient at first.
Perhaps he had his worries too—a wife and children? A
mortgage? A car that hadn't passed its MOT? She dozed
off without bothering to answer her own questions.

Two days later she packed her shoulder-bag, fastened
Podge into his basket and went home, a fairly simple
journey since the hospital was in the East End and on
the South Bank of the Thames; Waterloo Station was a
short bus ride away and there was a local train service
to Eynsford.

She sat in the train, one hand on Podge's basket, and
looked out at the Kent countryside, quiet and still green
under the autumn sun. One day, she promised herself,
she would leave London and get a post in a country
town—Canterbury, perhaps, Rochester, even Tunbridge
Wells, none of them too far away from her home. She

would have a Sister's post, of course... Her thoughts became woolly; she had been up all night and, even though she would have a nap when she got home, she still had to get there. She pulled her tired wits together as the train drew into the station, and got out.

Her father lived on the edge of the village. She passed the old Tollhouse at the junction of Sparepenny Lane with the road leading to the ford, and turned down a lane leading to a row of charming cottages. The end one was home; Emily went up the short garden path between the neglected flowerbeds and opened the solid wooden door.

Her father was sitting in his wheelchair, reading; with the kettle boiling its head off too. Emily put Podge's basket down, kissed her father, turned off the gas under the kettle and cast off her outdoor things.

Her father surveyed her with pleasure. 'What a delightful surprise, Emily! You're here for a few days?'

He couldn't disguise the eagerness in his voice and she answered quickly, 'Nights off, Father; four whole days after today. I'll make us a cup of coffee and you can bring me up to date with all the news. How are you?'

Mr Grenfell eyed her lovingly. 'Managing very well, my dear. Night duty finished? Have you been very busy?'

They exchanged their news over coffee while Podge, who had been there before, crept around reviving his memory of the place. Satisfied that it hadn't changed, he drank the saucer of milk he was offered and curled up on a chair in the sun.

Emily drank her coffee in sleepy content; it was lovely to be home again. She glanced round the comfortable, rather shabby room, at the comfortable chairs, the Welsh dresser with its complement of rather nice china plates and dishes, the balloon-backed chairs with their mid-Victorian seats which somehow looked quite right with the cricket table. The room was a hotch-potch of charming antique furniture, which, after years of being together, blended nicely. Emily's eye noted the dust under the dresser; after a good night's sleep she would give the cottage a thorough clean. Mrs Owen was a dear old thing and willing and very kind, but she had neither the time nor the strength to do more than tidy up each day.

Because she had wanted to talk about him ever since she had met him, Emily told her father about the man who had almost knocked her over on that wet and windy morning. She made a joke of it and joined in her father's amusement, but somewhere deep inside her that wistful longing to meet him again was definitely there. Only, she told herself, so that she could see if she liked him; after that she would forget him; he was too unsettling.

Not too difficult to forget him during the next day or two, as it turned out. Her days were full as she polished and Hoovered, dug the garden and weeded and played bezique with her father. She renewed friendships in the village too, with people who had known her since she was a little girl and who were full of kindly curiosity about her life in London. Emily answered them all in her friendly, matter-of-fact way, told them frankly that she had no young man and no prospect of one either, and lent a sympathetic ear to complaints of illness, naughty children and tiresome grandparents. Perhaps she should be a health visitor or something similar, she mused as she walked back home.

The evening before she went back to the hospital, she and her father had a talk. He had already told her that his arthritis was getting slowly worse, certainly more painful, and although he had made light of it, she sensed his worry.

'Would it be possible to mortgage the cottage?'

'My dear child, that's been done some years ago— your mother's illness...'

'There's nothing we can sell?'

'There would be very little money left by the time I'd redeemed the mortgage, my dear, and how could we afford to find a house to rent, or even a flat?' He added slowly, 'I could go into a geriatric ward...'

'Over my dead body!' declared Emily. 'Let's keep on as we are and hope for the best.'

She hated leaving her father. London, sprawling to meet her as she sat in the train, looked drab. She was aware that large parts of the city were elegant, with spacious squares and quiet streets lined with lovely old houses, and sometimes on her nights off she would take a bus to St Jame's Park, eat her sandwiches there, and then roam the neighbouring streets. A very different London from the one in which she worked and lived.

Back in hospital, the notice board informed her that she was to go to the Men's Orthopaedic Ward in six days' time—day duty, of course. Crowded round the notice as she and the other night nurses were on their way to the wards, she was surprised to hear cries of envy from such of her friends as were being posted at the same time.

'Emily, you lucky creature!' declared the pretty student nurse who was to report to Women's Surgical. 'You'll see that new consultant!'

Emily turned away from the noticeboard. 'You can have him as far as I'm concerned,' she observed matter-of-factly, 'though I like the idea of Orthopaedics.'

A nice change from the medical ladies, mostly chronic bronchitis, bad hearts and diabetes and, by the very nature of their illnesses, dispirited. Emily was a shy girl, but nursing a man was quite a different matter from socialising; she was completely at ease with her patients, but put them into their clothes and let her meet them away from their beds, outside the hospital, and she became a quiet, mouselike girl with no conversation. Yet she was liked at Pearson's; the students and the young housemen looked upon her as a rather silent sister, always ready to make cocoa or cut them a sandwich if they had been called out during the night. But none of them had ever asked her out.

Her last few nights on duty were busy ones; a sudden influx of elderly ladies with nasty chests, naturally enough sorry for themselves, anxious about husbands they had left to manage on their own, cats and dogs dependent upon neighbours and uncertain as to whether they had turned off the gas. Emily soothed and encouraged, listened endlessly to their worries and even, for one old lady, offered to go to her nearby flat and make sure that the canary was being properly fed. It made her late, which was why Mr van Tecqx saw her on the way home. He had walked to the hospital since it was a fine day and he was nearing it as she hurried down the street towards the Underground. She had a plastic bag under one arm and was so deep in thought that she didn't see him. She was, as she so often was, engaged in mental arithmetic.

She spent her nights off turning out her room and reading up Orthopaedics so that at least she would have some idea about that branch of nursing. The Sister on the ward was reputed to be an old tartar but a splendid

nurse. Even the more lively of her companions had declared that they would go anywhere but Orthopaedics,
although now that the mysterious consultant was there
they were prepared to change their ideas. Emily, if given
the chance, would quite cheerfully have exchanged a
posting with any one of them.

She climbed the staircase in plenty of time on her first
morning of day duty. Sister Cook set great store by
punctuality and, although she wouldn't be on duty until
half an hour after the nursing staff, she invariably asked
her staff nurses if there had been any latecomers.

In her first year, Emily had spent six weeks on the
women's side, but since she had had very little to do
with the actual treatment of the patients then, what
knowledge she had gleaned was of little use to her now.

Staff Nurse Ash was a large comforting type. 'You'll
soon get the hang of things,' she assured Emily. 'Don't
worry if Sister Cook blasts your head off, it's just her
way. We've just got time to go round the ward before
she comes on duty.'

All the beds were occupied and most of them had
various frames and cradles to support or protect the in-
mates' broken bones. They were a cheerful lot of men,
calling up and down the ward to each other, joking with
Staff Nurse Ash, and wishing Emily cheerful good
mornings. It was a far cry from Women's Medical; she
was going to like it.

She wasn't quite so sure an hour later. Sister Cook
was in a testy mood that morning; she disliked having
her nurses changed, and here was a girl who didn't look
capable of the quite heavy work she would be expected
to do. True, her reports from the other wards were good,
but she looked as if a strong breeze would knock her

down. Sister Cook, a big woman herself, rather despised the smaller members of her sex.

Over coffee in the canteen, Emily was questioned by her friends. They brushed aside her comments about Sister Cook and the patients; they wanted to know if the Dutch consultant had been on the ward, and if so, was he as marvellous as rumour had it?

Emily hadn't seen him. There had been a couple of housemen who had been friendly and there was a consultant's round at eleven o'clock, but she had no idea who was going to take it. With a customary eye on the clock she hurried back to the ward.

There was an hour before the round was due to start. Sister Cook marched up and down the ward, her hawklike eye searching out every small defect which might spoil the perfection of it. A junior nurse had already retired into the sluice room in tears, it just needed someone to trip over a Balkan Beam or drop a bowl; heaven forfend that she would be the one to do it, thought Emily with unhappy memories of the French consultant who had been so scathing about her clumsiness.

The ward clock pointed to eleven and the ward doors swung open. Sister Cook had taken up her position facing it; behind her stood the staff nurse, Nurse Ashe, and the junior staff nurse, both holding X-rays, Path Lab forms and all the paraphernalia necessary for the round, and behind them stood Emily, entrusted with a small trolley upon which were laid out, in an orderly fashion, the patients' notes.

It was a very good thing that they were laid out so neatly on the trolley, for when the door was thrust open and she saw who it was who came in, she would have dropped the lot if she had been holding on to them. The man who had almost knocked her down, no less, looking quite different in a dark grey suit of impeccable design, looming head and shoulders above the group of people milling about him; his Registrar, his housemen, medical students, the rather hearty lady from Physiotherapy and the social worker, the whole party swollen by Sister Cook, her staff nurses and Emily, trying to look as though she wasn't there. Not that she needed to worry; his gaze swept over her with no sign of recognition.

The round pursued its usual course with frequent pauses to assess a patient's mobility, lengthy arguments as to treatments, and even longer pauses while Mr van Tecqx listened patiently to the complaints, fears and doubts of the occupants of the beds. It took all of an hour, and the smell of the patients' dinners was strong from the ward kitchen as they all halted at the doors and polite exchanges were made before the consultant's posse moved off down the corridor.

'Nurse Grenfell, take the patients' charts back to my Office.' Sister Cook was already sailing in the opposite direction, intent on ticking off a patient who had had the temerity to complain to the consultant, of all people, about the breakfast porridge.

Emily escaped thankfully. It had been exciting meeting the man again, and thank heaven he hadn't recognised her, although it had been pretty mean of him to let her ramble on about her work when he was working at Pearson's himself.

She gained the office and started to stack the notes exactly as Sister liked them. She was almost finished when the door opened and Mr van Tecqx walked in.

Emily dropped the notes she was holding and said with a snap, 'There, look what you've made me do!' and then she remembered who she was talking to.

Her, 'Sorry, sir,' was polite but insincere, and she got down on to the floor and started to pick up the scattered sheets.

He got down beside her, taking up so much room that the Office seemed very small indeed. 'Surprised to see me?' he asked.

'Yes—well, yes, of course I am. I never imagined— you could have told me...' She took the papers from him and got to her feet. 'I'm not supposed to talk to you. Sister Cook will...'

'No, she won't,' He had taken the notes from her again and was arranging them tidily in their folder. 'Do you like this ward?'

'Yes, thank you, sir.'

He stared down at her, neat and rather prim. 'I can see that if we are to get anywhere conversationally, it will have to be away from this place. I'll be outside at eight o'clock this evening; we'll go somewhere and eat and exchange our life histories.'

Emily goggled up at his placid face. 'But we can't! Besides,' she added with some spirit, 'I haven't a life history.'

When he didn't say anything, only smiled at her, she went on, 'This just won't do, you know. I must go back on the ward...'

He opened the door for her. 'Eight o'clock,' he reminded her as she edged past him.

CHAPTER TWO

EMILY had no intention of doing anything of the sort; she told herself that a dozen times during the day. It was absurd anyway—how could she possibly go out with anyone in the elderly coat she wore to work? She would have had a long day and she would be tired and her hair would look awful. He must have been joking—but just to be on the safe side, she would go out through the side entrance. She would have to nip across the back of the entrance hall to reach it, but no one would see her.

All the same, she rushed back to her room during her three hours off after midday dinner, saw to Podge, washed her hair and, while it was drying, did her nails. Not because she had any intention of accepting Mr van Tecqx's surprising invitation, indeed she still wasn't sure if it was a joke. And she was far too busy to speculate about that during the evening; there were arms and legs to prepare ready for operation in the morning and supper to serve, and, since both staff nurses were off duty and she was on with Sister Cook, there was the added complication of keeping out of that lady's way as much as possible.

At length she was allowed to go, and skipped through the corridors and down the stairs to the cloakroom, where she bundled on her coat and with no thought as to her appearance, hurried down the back stairs to the back of the entrance hall. It was empty, although she could see Briggs' bald head in his lodge. Quelling a wish to go out of the entrance and have supper with Mr van Tecqx even as, she strongly suspected, he wouldn't be waiting for her, Emily nipped across the hall and opened the side door used by the staff and those fortunate enough to travel in their own cars.

The Bentley was parked exactly outside the door and Mr van Tecqx was leaning against its bonnet. Emily would have bounced back inside, only he was beside her before she could do so.

'I am much encouraged,' he told her, 'to find that we think alike—you, that you would escape by this door, and I quite certain of it. Come along, now, I'm hungry.'

Emily stood outside the door, his hand on her arm. 'Look, Mr van Tecqx, this really won't do—you're a consultant and I'm not even trained...'

A silly sort of remark, she realised as soon as she had uttered it. She tried again. 'I can't possibly go out with you in this.' She waved a hand at her coat.

'Well, of course you can't. I'll drive you to your lodgings and wait while you tidy yourself. You can have ten minutes; I've booked a table for half past eight.'

She made no effort to move. 'You were sure I would come?'

'No, that's why I waited here.' He smiled at her suddenly, which somehow made it perfectly normal to be going out to supper with him, although she was convinced that when she had the time to think about it she would be horrified. 'Student nurses just don't go out with consultants,' she voiced her thoughts out loud.

'There is always a first time.'

He popped her into the car and got in beside her.

Outside her gate she said, 'I'm sorry I can't ask you in—I've only got one room...'

For answer he got out of the car and went to open the door for her. 'Ten minutes,' he reminded her carefully.

Emily fed Podge, washed her face and made it up rather sketchily, then tore into her only decent dress—navy blue needlecord, bought in a C & A sale. Her coat was navy blue too, almost as elderly as the one she wore to work but neatly brushed and pressed. Her hair she brushed and tied back with a ribbon, as there was no time to pin it up. She thrust her feet into her one pair of high-heeled shoes, caught up her handbag and gloves, patted Podge and told him to be a good boy, and went out of the house followed by Mrs Winter's shrill voice.

'Got yerself a boyfriend, dearie? 'Ave a nice evening!'

If Mr van Tecqx heard her he gave no sign, merely remarked that punctuality was a virtue he seldom met with among his female acquaintances and stowed Emily into the car again.

He took her to Bubb's, just off the Farringdon Road and only a short distance away from Pearson's, and she was relieved to find that the people dining there were dressed very much as she was. The navy blue outfit, dull though it was, had the virtue of being inconspicuous. But she forgot to be shy in her companion's placid company; he talked as easily as anything about this and that, ordered her a sherry and told her to order what she fancied, and when she tried to make a bewildered choice, offered to do it for her: salmon mousse on a bed of lettuce, breast of chicken in an aspic glaze, accompanied by a variety of vegetables, followed by nougat glacé with strawberries and topped with cream.

The good food loosened her tongue, and, skilfully drawn out by her companion, Emily talked, something she hadn't done so freely with anyone for a very long time, but somehow her companion gave the impression of being a comfortable listener, putting questions just at the right moment, saying little. She was carried away, what with the delicacies which she was offered, the wine she was drinking and Mr van Tecqx's gentle interest. She was on the point of telling him her plans for her father when common sense took over and she stopped in mid-sentence.

Mr van Tecqx studied her face, on which a look of shocked wariness had settled. 'Yes?' he prompted softly.

'Oh, nothing—I can't remember what I was going to say, it wasn't in the least important. I hope I haven't bored you, Mr van Tecqx; this wine doesn't taste as strong as the bottle we got from the supermarket when Staff Nurse had her birthday... but I'm not used to drinking wine...'

Mr van Tecqx preserved an admirable calm. To anyone who compared Chablis Grand Cru at more than twenty pounds a bottle with something probably chosen because of its pretty label, he would have been scathing in his opinion of such gross ignorance, but all he did was agree with her blandly, and when she added in her sensible way, 'I'm afraid it made me talk too much,' said politely,

'Not at all, Emily—you don't mind if I call you Emily?'

She shook her head. 'Everyone does.' She hesitated. 'Why did you ask me to have dinner with you, Mr van Tecqx?'

'I'm a stranger in a strange land, and you have a kind appearance, Emily.'

It seemed to her that he was quite at home in London; his English was only very faintly accented, he knew his way around the city and if Staff Nurse was to be believed, he delivered scholarly lectures at hospitals other than Pearson's. She stared at him across the table. Because of the wine she had drunk his handsome features were slightly fuzzy round the edges, but even so, he was by far the most magnificent man she had ever met. She said now, 'You must have a great many friends.'

'Indeed, I have. Now, Emily, what was it you were going to tell me?'

'Oh, I can't remember...'

'About your father?' he prompted gently.

Her denial was instant, 'No, no, it wasn't anything...'

He had already discovered where she lived, now he observed, 'You must miss village life—Pearson's is situated in very drab surroundings. You look forward to your days off, I expect.'

Emily poured them more coffee. 'Oh, yes—only I don't go home each week.' She stopped again, her wretched tongue tripping along ahead of her wits. She expected him to ask, 'And why not?' Only he didn't, knowing that she wasn't going to tell him anyway.

He said easily: 'It is always a surprise to me that there is such charming country so close to London. Even in London itself—Hampstead and Richmond—one could almost be living in the country.'

She was on safe ground again; they did discuss London and its environs, until she said diffidently that she had to be in by eleven o'clock. 'I haven't an outdoor key, and Mrs Winter is very strict about us being in by then unless we make special arrangements.'

'There are other people living there?'

'Oh, yes, there are six rooms—she calls them flatlets and she's fussy about the tenants.'

'And you have a flatlet?'

There was no point in pretending. 'Well, no. Just a room—it's the attic really. But I've a sink and a little stove. It's quite cosy.' She uttered the lie cheerfully, relieved to see that he accepted it without comment, paid the bill and settled her in the car once more.

At her gate she said, 'Please don't get out—there's no need.'

A waste of breath, for he went with her up the path and opened the street door, to be confronted by Mrs Winter standing at the top of the basement stairs. 'There you are—I was jus' wondering?' She eyed Mr van Tecqx with belligerence. 'Me tenants 'as ter be in by eleven o'clock unless thcrc's an arrangement made.'

'Very wise,' said Mr van Tccqx. 'I am relieved to hear it. One cannot be too careful.' He looked down at Emily, standing silently beside him. 'Thank you for a delightful evening, Emily.'

She was very conscious of Mrs Winter's interested eyes. 'Thank you for my dinner, Mr van Tecqx, I enjoyed the evening very much. Goodnight.'

He answered her unsmilingly, bade Mrs Winter goodnight and went away, shutting the door quietly behind him. Mrs Winter secured the bolts.

'Wot did yer 'ave ter eat?' she asked.

Podge was waiting impatiently when Emily reached her room. She gave him his warm milk, got ready for bed and made a pot of tea while she told him about her evening. He sat, tidying his whiskers, his round eyes on her face, and when she observed in a puzzled voice, 'I can't think why he asked me out, Podge, even if he was lonely. I'm quite sure he must know lots of pretty girls with the right clothes...' he jumped on to her lap and butted her with his round head, offering a sympathy he felt was needed.

'Although,' went on Emily, thinking aloud, 'I ought to feel over the moon, oughtn't I?'

She got into bed, and with Podge curled up on her feet, went to sleep at once. In the morning, hurrying through the usual routine, the previous evening seemed like a distant dream.

That was how it was going to stay, she decided sensibly. She had let her tongue run away with her and told Mr van Tecqx far too much about herself, while he had remained reticent about himself. She blushed at the thought.

Even if she had wanted to, she was given no opportunity of saying so much as a 'Good morning, sir,' for the best part of the week. True, he appeared at his rounds, but she was not on duty for all of them, and when she was, she did no more than hand case sheets, hovering on the fringe of the group making its steady way from bed to bed, and once or twice when she had seen him as she hurried to the dispensary or the laundry at Sister's command it had seemed to her that he had deliberately not seen her. She had plenty of good sense; she told herself that it was only to be expected. Just because he had taken her out—no doubt on a sudden whim—it didn't mean to say that he had any interest in her. They didn't move in the same circles, a fact brought home to him when he had accompanied her to her lodgings. With good sense Emily bundled all thought of him to the back of her head, and even though his image popped out again far too often for her peace of mind, she thrust it back where it belonged—with her vague daydreams of the future.

The ward was full and a number of patients needed careful and constant nursing. Two burly young men who had fallen from a scaffolding on a high-rise block of flats had fractured spines, both with a degree of paralysis; they were nursed on ripple beds and had to be turned every two hours; no easy task and a continuous drain on the nurses' time, and, more than that, they had to be kept cheerful until such time as the paralysis should give way to the return of sensation. At the other end of the ward there was another young man recovering from the laminectomy which Mr van Tecqx had recently performed. A sprinkling of broken arms and legs and three fractured skulls made up the ward's inhabitants, most of them recovering nicely, but it was heavy work, and several times Emily saw Sister Cook looking at her in a thoughtful way, measuring her small person against the immovable arms and legs and backs and doubtless wondering if Emily would hold out. Which made Emily work all the harder, but it was worth it. She was learning as she worked, and even though she hadn't laughed all the way to the bank on pay-day, at least she smiled widely when she saw her nest-egg swell with the latest contribution.

What made it even more worth while was the discovery that one of the spinal fractures wiggled his toes as she was bed-bathing him. Even Sister Cook smiled at her and observed with slightly less acidity than usual that Emily had been most observant in her work. The Registrar was sent for and he in his turn requested the presence of Mr van Tecqx.

It was after he had finished his examination and expressed his opinion that his patient was on the mend, standing at the foot of the bed with Sister, his Registrar and, since Staff Nurse wasn't available, Emily, that he addressed her. 'You are to be commended for your sharp eyes, Nurse.' She gave a slight smile and he gave her a kindly smile as he walked away.

Emily went pink and a nearby patient with his leg slung up on a Balkan Beam said indignantly, 'Well, I'll be blowed! 'E could at least 'ave given you a pat on the shoulder, ducks.'

Emily gave him a severe look. 'Certainly not, Mr Crump, that wouldn't do at all—besides, any one of us could have been me.'

Upon which muddled speech she tucked him in with a brisk motherliness and started off down the ward. She was met half-way by one of the first-year nurses. 'Emily, you're to go to Sister's Office——' She paused to take a breath. 'He's there!'

'Who's he?' But Emily knew without being told. Was she going to be ticked off about something she should or should not have done? She was casting round anxiously in her mind as she pushed open the door of the Office to find Sister, Henry Parker, looking amused, and Mr van Tecqx, looking bland.

It was Sister who spoke. 'Nurse Grenfell, Mr van Tecqx has made a suggestion to me which I'm sure will gratify you. It seems that he has to drive past your home on your day off—tomorrow—and offers to give you a lift. It's most kind of him, and I'm sure you will be delighted to accept his most generous offer.'

Emily cast a quick look at him. He was gazing out of the window at the vista of chimneypots, just as though the conversation had nothing to do with him. She felt tempted to refuse since his offer, given second-hand as it were, held no vestige of interest, but on the other hand an unexpected chance to go home wasn't to be missed. She said with polite woodenness, 'Thank you, Sister, I shall be most grateful to have a lift home.'

Mr van Tecqx turned away from his scrutiny of the hospital's environment. There was a faint tremor at the corners of his firm mouth which might have been the beginnings of a smile. 'My pleasure, Nurse. No doubt Sister will be kind enough to give you the details at her convenience.'

Sister Cook gave a regal nod. 'Certainly, sir. You may go, Nurse.'

Emily went.

She had to wait until the evening, when she was about to go off duty, before Sister Cook sailed down the ward towards her. 'Trouble on the way,' warned a patient *sotto voce*. The patients liked her, she was such a scrap of a thing and yet nothing was too much trouble for her. She pinched out a cigarette from a patient's hand and turned a calm face to her superior.

'I smell smoke,' declared Sister Cook, and cast a suspicious look around her. She allowed smoking on the ward, but only at hours dictated by herself.

'It's always rather smoky at this time in the evening,' volunteered Emily in her calm way. 'I suppose it's all the chimneys and people coming home from work. Shall I close the windows, Sister?'

Sister Cook had a thing about fresh air, even though it wasn't all that fresh in that part of London. She said no quite sharply and added, 'I have a message for you, Nurse Grenfell. Mr van Tecqx will be outside your flat a half past eight in the morning. Don't keep him waiting, Nurse. He's a busy man.'

Emily was ready and waiting when she saw the car stop before her lodgings in the morning. She picked up her overnight bag, took a grip of Podge's basket, and went down to the front door. Mr van Tecqx was on the step, searching in vain for a bell or a knocker. She wished him good morning politely and he said sharply, 'For heaven's sake stop calling me Sir with every other breath!'

She got into the car and watched him stow Podge on the back seat. 'Why ever not?' she asked him. 'I'm expected to do so.'

'Not by me, you're not, not when we are away from Pearson's. I must say I find it very tiresome having to ignore you or at best look through you when I'm on my rounds.'

A remark which surprised Emily so much that she stayed silent while he settled beside her and drove off. As though he had read her thoughts he went on, 'If I were to show the least sign of interest in you, Sister Cook would pounce. In her eyes, consultants and student nurses don't mix; the fact that they are men and women as well has no bearing on the matter from her point of view.'

Emily said, 'Oh, yes,' rather inadequately.

'So next time I ignore you on the ward you will know why.'

She sought for a suitable reply and came up with, 'Oh—really?'

She heard him sigh and sought for a topic of conversation. Manners mattered, her mother had always told her, and she had always tried to remember that. 'Are you going to Dover?' she asked.

'No—I have friends in Biddenden.'

The silence lasted a little too long. Emily tried again. 'The country around there is charming, and Biddenden is charming too...'

They were going down the A20 towards Swanley; the road was moderately free from traffic and Mr van Tecqx was driving fast. 'Tell me about your father?' he invited.

'My father?' repeated Emily stupidly. 'What do you mean—what do you know about him? I never...'

'My dear girl, I have ways of finding out the things I wish to know. How long has he been waiting for hip replacements?'

Emily ignored him. 'What do you know about my father—how dare you snoop...?'

'My dear girl, I never snoop—I have no need to do so. I had occasion to discuss a patient with your father's doctor and in the course of conversation mentioned that you were a nurse at Pearson's and that he might know you. He told me of your father's condition.'

Emily cast him a quick look. His profile was calm, his voice had been uninterested, there was no reason to doubt his word. She said reluctantly: 'I'm sorry. He's been waiting for more than a year and it will be another year before there's a bed for him.'

'That is the National Health?' asked Mr van Tecqx gently.

'Yes.' She hesitated. 'As a matter of fact, I found out how much it would cost for him to be a private patient— it would save a year of waiting.'

'So he will go privately?'

'Well, yes...'

'As soon as you have saved the money?' Mr van Tecqx's voice was so quiet she barely heard it.

'Yes.'

He nodded. 'Do you know your doctor's number?'

'Yes, of course.'

'Then ring him up now on the car phone, will you, and ask him to meet us at your father's house in—let me see—half an hour's time.'

Emily made no move to do as he had asked. 'Why?'

'Let us not waste time. Your GP can call me in for consultation—I'll have a look at your father and see what can be done.'

She said a little wildly, 'But there are no beds—I asked. Two years, they said, and I haven't saved enough money.'

'The phone, Emily.' His voice held a note she didn't care to argue with. She did as she was bidden and then sat silent until they reached Eynsford.

'You have to go up Sparepenny Lane and past the Tollhouse—it's the row of cottages a bit further on,' she told him.

Dr Mason was already there. Emily kissed her father, was greeted cheerfully by the doctor and introduced Mr van Tecqx, who nodded at the doctor, remarking that they were acquainted, and then shook hands with her father.

Her father was not in the least surprised to see him. Dr Mason, he explained to Emily, had arranged it all and he for his part was delighted. 'Although I dare say I shall still have another year or two to wait, but just to be told by you, Mr van Tecqx, that there's a possibility of success is a great encouragement.'

Emily, swamped in the unexpectedness of it all and vaguely suspicious at the same time, allowed her parent to suggest that she might go along to the kitchen and make coffee for everyone. 'And don't hurry back,' begged Mr Grenfell. 'We can manage very nicely.'

Emily gave Mr van Tecqx a speaking glance and did as she was told. Matters for the moment at least, were out of her hands.

There was plenty to do in the kitchen. She arranged a tray, ground the coffee and set it in the old percolator on to the gas stove. Mrs Owen had been that morning, for the dishes were washed and stacked neatly, but the sink needed a good scrub and her idea of cleaning the floor wasn't Emily's. Emily took off her outdoor things, donned an apron and set to work. She was washing her hands at the now pristine sink when her father called to her to bring in the coffee. She had got a little untidy as she worked, but beyond tucking a stray lock of hair behind an ear, she had no time for more; she bore in the tray which Mr van Tecqx took for her and set on the table under the window.

It was very vexing that the three men were discussing cricket and showed no sign of changing the conversation. She handed out cups, sugar and biscuits and sat composedly, seething inwardly. It seemed a long time before Dr Mason put down his cup and saucer, declared that he still had the rest of his patients to see and he would leave them all to make the arrangements. He shook Mr Grenfell's hand, gave Emily a friendly pat on the back with the injunction to be a good girl, then shook hands with Mr van Tecqx. 'Give me a ring when you're ready and I'll fix things this end. I'm greatly obliged to you, Sebastian.'

Emily, itching to hear what they had all been discussing, was momentarily diverted by the idea of Mr van

Tecqx being called Sebastian. She wondered if his friends called him Seb and decided that they wouldn't dare—he would fix them with a glare from the blue eyes which were almost always half hidden by heavy lids. She studied him from where she sat. He must be around thirty-five, she supposed; his fair hair had a good deal of silver in it . . .

He had turned his head to look at her and she went bright pink and looked away, wishing fervently that she didn't blush so easily.

'I must admire your patience, Emily.' He came and sat down between her and her father. 'I think we might operate on your father within the next week or so.'

She sat up very straight. 'But I—where will he go? Sister said there wasn't a bed for months . . .' She looked at her father. 'Father, do explain!'

'Well, dear, I think Mr van Tecqx can do that better than I. I shall leave it to him.'

'Ah, yes—Emily, if you will walk with me to the car we can settle matters easily enough.'

Out of her father's hearing she said urgently, 'I don't understand, and there you were talking about cricket . . . it's all very well stating you'll operate. Don't think I'm ungrateful, but you don't understand—it'll have to be private, of course, and the thing is I haven't saved enough money—it will be at least four or five months, and you might not be here then.'

'No, I shan't. Your father can have a bed in a private hospital where I sometimes send patients, and I will operate there, and he can convalesce in a rest home—there is a good one just outside Richmond.'

Emily stopped herself just in time from wringing her hands. 'But you don't understand!' They were standing by the car and she stared up anxiously into his face.

'If you would just trust me, Emily. I have to go—I'm already late—but I shall come for you tomorrow evening and I will explain. There will be no question of fees, but I want to strike a bargain with you. More about that later.' With which infuriatingly unhelpful remark he got into his car and drove off.

Her father was just as unhelpful, not meaning to be but wanting to discuss every aspect of the operation and what it would mean in the future.

'I must say,' he observed happily to Emily, 'it's extremely good of Mr van Tecqx to make an operation possible. It seems he has beds at his disposal at some private hospital and the opportunity to operate before he returns to Holland. I mentioned fees, but he said he'd come to some arrangement with you, my dear. I dare say you can pull a few strings with the National Health people?' He gave a chuckle. 'Nursing must have its perks!'

Emily agreed cheerfully. There was no point in voicing her doubts and it was really wonderful to see her father so happy.

It was impossible to worry all the time. She cooked and cleaned and shopped in the village, then went for a rambling walk to go home in the gathering dusk to cook their supper and feed Podge, and her simple chores soothed her so that by the time Mr van Tecqx arrived at the gate she was prepared to hear whatever it was that he wanted to say.

He had arrived earlier than she had expected—he had said he would fetch her in the evening, but it was barely four o'clock and she had just made the tea. Probably he had a date in town, she decided, and invited him to have a cup of tea which she assured him was ready, and she was also quite ready to leave.

When he had drunk his tea and eaten a good deal of the cake she had made he still made no move to go. Instead, much to Emily's surprise, he suggested that she might accompany him on a brief walk. 'There are things which I have to say to you,' he concluded.

'Oh, well—all right. But don't you have to get back to town? I thought that as you were here so early...' She faltered at the smile and amused look on his face.

'Of course I have to get back—so do you; that's why I'm here so early.'

He waited patiently while she got her coat, tied a scarf around her head and made sure that her father was comfortable, and then accompanied him down the path and into the lane.

'Somewhere quiet?' he suggested.

'Down the lane to the end; there's a bridle path we can take, it will bring us out on the other side of the Tollhouse—about twenty minutes or so.'

'Excellent.'

He had nothing to say for a minute or so and she prompted him with, 'You want to strike a bargain?'

He was walking at his own pace, so that she had difficulty in keeping up with him. 'Yes. I'm prepared to operate upon your father—both hips—within the next week or two. Neither I nor the anaesthetist nor the private hospital where I propose he should be will require fees, although I do ask something in return. I have a young sister—the youngest of four—nineteen years old. She contracted polio last year and is making a slow recovery—too slow for her. She is impatient, given to bouts of rage and fits of depression. She is wearing my mother down, and a succession of nurses come and go with predictable rapidity. She needs someone of her own age, someone calm and kind and patient and at the same time firm. She is a dear girl, make no mistake, and she will make an almost complete recovery; but at the moment she has stopped trying; she needs something new to get her going again. Do I make myself clear?'

'Oh, perfectly.' They were walking along the bridle path side by side. 'But, Mr Van Tecqx, I'm not trained— I have another year to do. I'm not free, even if I wanted to be.'

'I can arrange that.'

'I have no doubt of that,' Emily's voice was dry. 'But what about me? Am I to start all over again once your sister is well again?'

'No. I think it can be arranged that you will need to do only an extra six months to complete your training after you have done your third year.'

'And if I don't agree?' She stopped to look at him. 'You won't operate?'

His voice was silky. 'My sister is very dear to me, Emily, and I imagine that your father is also dear to you. It amounts to this: You will help me and I shall help you.'

'Yes, but there must be dozens of nurses who would do just as well as I would.'

'Probably. Do you know dozens of surgeons who are willing to operate upon your father? Just think, Emily; within a few months he will have the use of his legs again; he will be able to walk to the village, go for rambles, even get a part-time job if he wishes—drive a car...'

'It's blackmail,' she said fiercely.

He agreed blandly. 'What is more, you will have to trust me completely, Emily. I give you my word that everything needful will be done for your father and that when, eventually, you are ready to return to nursing, you will be given every opportunity to take your exams at the earliest possible moment.'

They had gained the lane once more and were passing the Tollhouse; in another five minutes they would be back at her home. 'Podge,' said Emily suddenly.

'I have a housekeeper who looks after me when I am in London. Would you consent to her looking after Podge while you are away?'

'He might run away.'

'Mrs Twig will take great care of him. He is not a very adventurous cat, is he? He has known hard times and he isn't likely to leave a comfortable home.'

She said sharply, 'You make it all sound so easy.'

'As it is.' They had arrived back at the cottage and had paused outside its door.

'How long will it take—the operation on Father and then his convalescence?'

'He will be on his feet by Christmas.'

'And your sister?'

'That will depend largely on you. But you have my word that the moment she is able to cope with life once more, you shall return to England. You will, of course, be paid a salary; you will not suffer financially.'

Emily was back at her old habit of doing sums in her head. She wouldn't need to touch her savings—once she got back home she and her father would be able to have a holiday, a decent one at a hotel with no cheeseparing, and she would be able to live at the hospital again. She drew a deep breath. 'All right, I'll do it.'

He held out a large hand and she put hers into it. Probably she would wake up in the night and regret what she was doing, but just at that moment the whole plan seemed very sensible and easy, and above all, exactly what she had hoped for for her father.

'I shall operate at the end of next week; your father will have limited walking exercise after twenty-four hours, his stitches will come out after a week or ten days and he will be home again before three weeks. The joint should be normal at the end of three months. I'll do the second hip then.'

'Yes, but who's going to look after him? I won't be at home, will I? He can't stay in the hospital for months!'

'I know just the person to look after him. If you will agree, she can move in and look after your father. A retired nurse, middle-aged and a very good cook.'

'But it will all cost so much—I mean, even without your fees.'

'Ah, you forget, I shall deduct an agreed sum from your salary while you are looking after my sister.' He smiled suddenly. 'Trust me, Emily, I'm not offering you charity! You will pay for it—probably more than you bargain for—my sister won't be easy. There is still time for you to change your mind.'

She shook her head. 'I shan't do that. You see, it's something I've wanted so badly for a long time—to have my father back on his feet again. I'll do my best with your sister, really I will.'

'I know that. Shall we tell your father the plans? He will probably have plans of his own to work out.'

'Yes, all right. Do you want to leave as soon as possible?'

'Well, I was rather hoping that I might share your supper.' He contrived to sound both hungry and lonely. 'I'll talk to your father while you cook.'

A couple of hours later, sitting beside Mr van Tecqx, being driven back to Pearson's, Emily did her best to gather her scattered wits together into some sort of order. It all sounded so easy when he talked about it, but she saw snags at every turn. 'Do I have to go to the office?' she asked suddenly.

'Eventually, but I will see the Senior Nursing Officer tomorrow morning; she will send for you, I dare say. You would like to stay till your father is home again, wouldn't you? I can arrange for you to leave in about three weeks' time, you will be able to see him settled with Mrs Philips. Don't worry about getting to Holland; I will deal with that and then let you know.' Emily stirred restlessly and he added quietly, 'Just take one thing at a time, Emily.'

When they reached her digs, he got out of the car, took her overnight bag from her, opened the front door and went in with her. In the narrow hall with Mrs Winter's door open a crack so that she could hear every word, Emily said hastily, 'Thank you for the lift, Mr van Tecqx.'

'I'm coming up, just to see you safely in.' He had raised his voice deliberately. 'You can't manage Podge and your bag.'

He stood beside her in her room, taking in its shabbiness and not saying a word. But when he turned to go he paused and dropped a kiss on her cheek. She uttered a surprised goodnight to an empty room.

CHAPTER THREE

EMILY lay awake far too long, thinking about Mr van Tecqx's kiss. It had been a chaste salute but a kiss nevertheless; she had a nasty feeling that it was because he pitied her living in a poky attic.

In consequence she had overslept, so that she had had to hurry over her dressing and sketchy breakfast, attend to Podge and then hurry through the streets to the Underground. The day went wrong from the start. Sister Cook was in a bad mood, finding fault with everyone and everything. Emily was off duty at five o'clock, but long before that she would have given a great deal to have bolted from the ward and rushed home to Podge's undemanding company. It was mid-afternoon when Sister Cook sent for her.

'You're to go to the office at once,' she stated. 'I have no idea why, but it's highly inconvenient. How I'm expected to run this ward with half the trained nurses for ever going to the office, I don't know!'

Emily said meekly, 'Yes, Sister,' and sped away. Mr van Tecqx might have given Sister Cook a hint; now she would have to report back from the Office and explain why she was leaving. Her tired brain really couldn't cope with it. She tapped on the SNO's door and was bidden to enter.

The SNO was a good deal easier than Sister Cook. She appeared to find nothing strange in Mr van Tecqx's request that Emily should leave within a few weeks in order to nurse his sister. Emily was not of course to know that the SNO was an old friend of his mother... She said, 'Yes, Miss Webb!' and 'No, Miss Webb, when necessary and got herself out of the office. There were no obstacles put in the way of her leaving and she might return if she wished and finish her training, but she doubted very much if Sister Cook would see things in the same light. She went back to the ward, took a deep heartening breath, and tapped on Sister's door.

Sister Cook was seated at her desk and Mr van Tecqx was leaning against a wall, looking what Emily could only think of as smug.

Sister's voice, pitched fortissimo for most of the day, was surprisingly dulcet. 'Ah—yes, Nurse Grenfell. Mr van Tecqx has been explaining to me that you're exactly the nurse that he would wish for his sister. I've agreed that you should leave in two weeks' time, and should you decide to return to finish your training here later on, I for one can see no objection.'

Emily didn't look at Mr van Tecqx; he had obviously been laying on the charm, and pretty thickly too. She said, 'Yes, Sister, thank you,' in her calm way, and stood waiting to be told to go.

'Mr van Tecqx tells me he has to make known his arrangements to you before he returns to Holland. You'll go off duty at five o'clock punctually, Nurse Grenfell, so that you may be briefed.'

Emily said, 'Yes, Sister,' once again, and, told to go, went.

It was all very well, she thought as she went off duty, but who was to brief her, and where? Perhaps there would be a letter for her at the lodge. She went to the entrance hall and, although there was no letter, Mr van

Tecqx was there instead, leaning against the lodge, reading the evening newspaper.

He folded it neatly when he saw her, handed it back to the porter and went to meet her.

'I am sorry that I cannot ask you out this evening, but I have a prior engagement. I intend to operate upon your father in four days' time.' He paused to study her calm face, wreathed in rather untidy mousy hair. He mentioned the private hospital, not too far away from Pearson's. 'You will be able to visit every day, and by the time you leave here he should be very nearly fit to go back home. You will be able to go there, will you not, and be nicely settled in by the time he returns with the nurse? I should be glad if you would hold yourself in readiness to go to Holland within a few days of his return.' He waited for her to speak, but as she said nothing he continued. 'I have been thinking about Podge. Perhaps if you agree, it would be pleasanter for him if he were to go to your home? He's not a complete stranger to it, is he, and he will be company for your father—and you will have regular news of him...?'

'Thank you, that sounds a good idea. How will Father get to this hospital?'

'I will arrange that. I have asked Sister Cook to let you have days off so that you can be there when I operate.'

Emily said gratefully, 'You've thought of everything. Thank you very much.'

'Reserve your thanks, Emily, I suspect you will be getting the worst of the bargain.'

She shook her head. 'Oh, no. How can you say that? What could be worse than Father having to sit in a wheelchair for years?'

'I'll tell you—my young sister, bursting with impatience and taking it out on the nearest person—you, Emily.'

'But she will get better?'

'Yes, and that will depend largely upon you.' He glanced at the thin gold watch on his wrist. 'I have to go. I'll see that you are kept informed.'

Emily stood watching him go through the door. He really was a very large man, she reflected, as his broad shoulders disappeared into the gathering dark outside. She wondered briefly where he was going and what kind of life he had away from the hospital, before going to the cloakroom to get her outdoor things and take herself off home.

She had thought that the next couple of weeks would go slowly, but instead of that she discovered that she was occupied with a dozen small chores which had to be done before she left the hospital and her room. Mrs Winter had been surprisingly upset when Emily had told her she was leaving, and went to the trouble of rooting around in the basement for an old trunk she no longer needed and was prepared to sell to Emily for a modest sum. It was a ramshackle thing, but in her year or two at Pearson's Emily had acquired bits and pieces for her room which she was loath to discard. She packed, paid her modest bill, and waited for whatever would happen next.

Mr van Tecqx had made no effort to contact her at Pearson's. He had done his ward rounds as usual, wishing her good morning if he encountered her, thanking her politely if it should fall to her lot to hand him a patient's chart or X-ray; the last day came and she was none the wiser as to her future.

Her father had had his operation. Emily had spent her days off at the hospital where he was a patient. Someone there had phoned her and given her the time of the operation and suggested that she might like to be at the hospital while it took place, and they had been kind to her there, settling her in a comfortable waiting-room, bringing her tea and coffee and sandwiches, and when finally they told her that the operation was over, Mr van Tecqx had come to find her, still in his green cotton smock and trousers, to assure her that it had been entirely successful and that she might see her father very shortly. She had spent most of the next day there too, delighted to find her father on his feet, if only for a few painful moments, and after that she had visited each day when she was off duty, and now he had been considered fit enough to return home with his nurse. But first she was to go home and have everything in readiness. Presumably she would be contacted once she was home and her father was settled in.

It was a wrench leaving Pearson's and her chance to qualify in a year's time, but she had the good sense not to give way to self-pity. She had got her wish, and sooner than she had hoped. In six months or so she would be able to complete her training. Her friends frankly envied her even while they wished her the best of luck, and even Sister Cook managed a wintry smile. For the last time Emily went along the passages and down the stairs to the cloakroom to get her coat, carrying a plastic bag bulging with an assortment of gifts from both patients and friends.

She was crossing the entrance hall when the porter called her. There was a note, he told her, delivered half an hour ago.

She knew the unreadable writing—Mr van Tecqx had remembered her.

She would be picked up on the following morning at nine o'clock. Would she kindly have her luggage and Podge ready at that time? It was a businesslike note, signed with his initials. And just suppose I'd made my own arrangements, reflected Emily, what would I have done? To whom would I have applied?

She lost no time in tucking the note tidily away and going back to her room, now looking bare and unlived-in. She fed a peevish Podge, stowed her presents in the trunk and opened a can of beans before taking a bath and going to bed. It would be lovely to be home again, even if only for a few days, and despite Mr van Tecqx's rather gloomy account of his sister, she was looking forward to her new job. Indeed, she had the good sense to realise that there wasn't much point in doing otherwise.

She was up betimes, eating a hasty breakfast, feeding Podge and packing the last of her things and then taking her luggage downstairs to the narrow hall. The trunk took a good deal of manhandling even with Mrs Winter to help, but she was ready and waiting by nine o'clock, when, exactly on time, Mr van Tecqx drew up before the sagging gate. He cast a thoughtful eye over Emily's bits and pieces and then began to load her cases, plastic bags and Podge into the back of the car; to her offer to help with the trunk he made no answer but heaved it into the boot without any fuss, bade her get into the car, wished Mrs Winter goodbye, got inside beside Emily and drove off.

'I didn't know it would be you,' said Emily.

'How should you, since I had not said so,' observed Mr van Tecqx so austerely that she stayed silent for quite five minutes.

'You're operating at half past eleven,' she reminded him. 'I saw the list last night.'

'Yes, I know—they do let me see the list too.' The hint of sarcasm blended with the austerity and she winced.

'I have no wish to pry,' she told him kindly. 'I just wouldn't like you to be delayed.' She glanced at his rather stern profile and was struck by a sudden thought. 'Have you been up all night?'

'Not all night—since half past three.'

'You should have told me—I could have caught the train...' She paused, because in view of her pile of possessions it just wouldn't have been possible. 'Mrs Winter could have sent my luggage later...'

'If by luggage you mean that deplorable collection of plastic bags and whatever which I have loaded into the car, they wouldn't have got far.'

Emily said haughtily, 'I can't afford Gucci luggage.'

He laughed. 'Don't be peevish!'

'I am not peevish.' She did her best to keep her voice well modulated and reasonable. After all, he was quite right about her luggage. And he had been up most of the night too...

They travelled in silence, although Podge, fed up in his basket, mumbled and grumbled to himself. They were more than half-way there when Mr van Tecqx spoke. 'I intend to go back to Holland in four days' time. I hope that you will accompany me. I shall not be free until the afternoon of that day, so it will be necessary to take a night ferry. Kindly be ready to go with me. I will come for you not later than half past six.'

'Father...' began Emily.

'Will be quite all right. I would not ask you to leave him otherwise.'

'Very well, I shall be ready.' She drew a breath. 'Mr van Tecqx, I haven't thanked you properly for all you've done for Father and me. I'm very grateful; life is suddenly quite different...'

She didn't see the little smile. 'There I must agree with you, although for me it is for quite another reason.'

'Oh, well, I expect so—I mean, you're going back home, aren't you?' She paused, getting what she wanted to say exactly right. 'By the time you'll want to operate on Father's other hip I shall have enough money saved to pay your fees...'

She was brought up short by his curt, 'That will do, Emily. We made a bargain, you and I, we will keep to our side of it. I wish to hear no more about it.'

She said reasonably, 'Well, I dare say you don't, but you have no need to sound so annoyed, although I expect it's because you haven't had enough sleep.'

He uttered a crack of laughter at that but said nothing—indeed, he had nothing more to say, not even when he drew up before the cottage.

He got out and opened the door for her. Cross he might be, she reflected, but he hadn't forgotten his manners. She went up the little path and opened the door, then went back to fetch Podge in his basket and some of the plastic bags. As Mr van Tecqx dumped the trunk in the tiny hall she asked, 'You'll have a cup of coffee? I'll be very quick. Did you have breakfast?'

What with the trunk and the pair of them there was hardly room to move. Emily looked up into his face and saw the tired lines in it. She answered for him, 'Scrambled eggs on toast—you can eat that quickly.'

She didn't wait for him to answer but went to the kitchen and filled the kettle and got down a saucepan for the eggs. Only when that was done did she stop to let Podge out of his basket and invite Mr van Tecqx to sit down. The little house was cold, but the sun shone, and once she had cut the bread and fetched the milk and butter, she lit the gas fire in the sitting room. 'I'll bring the tray in here,' she told him. 'About five minutes— I'll be as quick as I can.'

'Anxious to be rid of me?' he wanted to know, and took off his coat and pulled his chair nearer the fire. 'It's not yet half past ten. May I use your telephone?'

While she stirred the eggs carefully, she heard him telling someone—his Registrar, she supposed—that he might be half an hour late.

She carried the tray in presently and found him asleep. She put it down silently and stood looking at him. He appeared a lot younger somehow and quite different from the rather austere consultant who visited the ward; rather as though he had taken off a mask.

He opened his eyes and the mask slipped back into place.

Emily poured their coffee and nibbled toast while he ate his eggs. Rather diffidently, she offered him some more toast and he ate that too.

'Is the list very long?' she asked, absurdly visualising him dropping off to sleep over a fractured leg.

'Not too bad. A laminectomy, a spina bifida, a crushed foot which should have been seen to days ago—the man didn't get his doctor until he could no longer stand the pain—oh, and a malignant tumour, a child of twelve. I do hope we can do something for him.'

Emily said worriedly: 'You really shouldn't have brought me, you need your rest and you'll be operating for hours.'

'Ah, but you are restful, Emily—and don't worry, if I'm tired, I don't operate.'

He went soon afterwards, driving away, relaxed and at ease. To look at him, she thought, he gave the impression of a man who had slept all night. She watched the Bentley disappear down the lane and then went indoors; she was conscious of feeling lonely, but there was plenty to do before her father arrived on the following day.

Mrs Owen had been in each week to keep an eye on things, but Emily went through the cottage like a small whirlwind, Hoovering and polishing, making beds and finally making a cake for the next day before getting her own supper and dealing with Podge. Tomorrow, she decided, she would get up early and clean the vegetables Mrs Owen had left for her, pop down to the village for a chicken and find some flowers for Mrs Philips's room. She was in bed before ten o'clock, tired out but happy, with Podge lying heavily on her feet. Just before she dropped off she wondered sleepily if Mr van Tecqx had got through his day in a satisfactory manner. 'Well, of course he has,' she muttered to an uncaring Podge. 'I don't suppose he's ever been flummoxed by anything or anyone.' Naturally enough Podge didn't reply, and she rolled into a comfortable ball and went to sleep.

The telephone rang while she was having breakfast to tell her that her father would be leaving the hospital at eleven o'clock. Emily recognised the voice—it belonged to the very pretty Ward Sister who had been in charge of her father, and who, Emily hadn't failed to notice, was on excellent terms with Mr van Tecqx; always very correct and professional in her manner, of course, but there had been the quick glance and fleeting smile and, although he had made no sign, Emily was very sure that he was pleasurably aware of them. Well, good luck to them, she thought, gobbling the last of her toast, her mind already half full of the morning's chores. Mr van Tecqx was no longer a young man—not old either, but all the same he might find his life more comfortable with a wife. She paused as she opened a tin of cat food for Podge. Perhaps he already had one, living in Delft, because that was where he had told her his home was.

It was a joy to see her father walking with a crutch and with Mrs Philips in close attendance, coming slowly up the garden path. She went to meet him and he gave her a warm kiss.

'I never thought I'd do this again,' he told her. 'You have no idea, Emily, how marvellous this is.'

He was managing very well, Mrs Philips told her. 'Still a good deal of pain from the other hip, but Mr van Tecqx will attend to that in due course.'

She was a pleasant, rather stout woman, in her late fifties perhaps, but not looking that, and her father liked her, Emily could see that with relief. They had coffee in the sitting-room with the two ambulance men and then she took Mrs Philips to show her her room.

'It's not very large, I'm afraid, but there's a lovely view...'

'Bless you, my dear, it's delightful. Don't you worry about your father, I'll take good care of him. He's doing splendidly—Mr van Tecqx thinks he'll be able to do the other hip in two months. By the spring your father will be walking with the best of us.' She glanced at Emily's happy face. 'You'll be going over to Holland, he tells me, to nurse his sister back on to her feet—a bit of a handful, apparently. A real family man, he is. A pity his wife died.'

'Oh, was he married? How sad for him. Hasn't he any children?'

'No, and him so fond of them, too.' Mrs Philips sighed. 'Such a nice man too! A bit reserved, you might say, and fussy about his patients; keeps himself to himself, as it were. I dare say all you young nurses did your best to catch his eye...'

'Well, yes—the pretty ones, you know, but I don't think he bothered much, not at Pearson's.' Emily remembered the pretty Sister who had looked after her father and decided that she didn't want to talk about him any more. 'I've written down the ordinary things you might want to know without bothering my father— you know, the tradespeople and the milkman and where you can get the eggs. I do so hope you'll like it here.'

'I'm sure I shall. You've no idea how long you'll be in Holland, have you?'

'None at all. It all depends, doesn't it? I'd like to be home for Christmas, but I shan't bank on that. Are you in a hurry to leave, Mrs Philips?'

'No, my dear. I'm a widow, I've got a son in Canada; he'll be coming home some time next year and until then I shall keep on with private nursing.'

Emily said rather shyly, 'Did Mr van Tecqx tell you we only have Mrs Owen from the village to clean? She comes twice a week when I'm home, but when I was in hospital she popped in each day just to tidy up.'

'Mr van Tecqx explained about that. I'll enjoy some housekeeping—looking after your father won't take all that time.'

'You won't mind looking after Podge, will you?'

'I love cats. If you're in Holland for some time, I dare say you'll be able to come over for a few days to see how we're all getting on.'

'You're awfully kind, Mrs Philips. I—I hate leaving Father, but I promised Mr van Tecqx... He's been very good to me.'

'He's a good man, Emily. Likes his own way, of course, but what man doesn't?'

They smiled at one another with mutual approval and went back to where her father was sitting by the fire, reading his post. He looked up as they went in, smiling. 'I feel a new man, you can have no idea... I saw Mr van Tecqx this morning before I left the hospital, and he told me that he plans to do the other hip in eight weeks' time. I can hardly believe my good fortune! And you, Emily, I have to thank you too—you have no objection to going to Holland, have you? It will be an experience.'

'I shall enjoy it very much, Father.' Emily's voice was as serene as ever; any doubts she had she intended to keep to herself. A host of them had crept into her head now that she was on the point of going to Holland. Her patient might dislike her on sight, Mr van Tecqx's family might feel the same, and were they all as coolly bent on having their own way with everything? He hadn't mentioned her free time. Would she get any, living with the family, and would her clothes be right? She had meant to go to the public library and read up all about Delft, but somehow there had not been the time. She had seen pictures of it, of course, and it looked charming; she would write long letters to her father and her friends at Pearson's and describe everything. She had no idea exactly where Mr van Tecqx lived in the little city; since he was a surgeon she presumed he would have consulting rooms there, but perhaps he lived in one of its suburbs... Well, she would soon know.

The intervening days passed too quickly. The last day came and Emily packed, prudently putting in two new blue overalls with neat white collars and cuffs, just in case she was expected to look like a nurse. She and Mrs Philips had had pleasant discussions over innumerable pots of tea concerning her father's treatment, what he liked to eat, a brief résumé on the village shops and Podge's diet, and there was, she felt, nothing more to be said or done. She was sitting waiting in her brown winter coat which she had decided would have to do for another winter; it was well cut but out of date and the colour did nothing for her, and Mr van Tecqx's rather cold eyes slid over her with polite indifference. Not that she minded, she reflected, only very slightly put out; hadn't she got her wish and wasn't her father standing there, showing off his new hip joint?

Mr van Tecqx accepted coffee and a slice of the fruit cake Emily had made that morning, but he wasted no time. He examined her father briefly, had a few words with Mrs Philips and picked up Emily's case.

'Is this all?' he wanted to know, and then with the faintest sneer, 'No plastic bags?'

She ignored that; he had kept his side of their bargain, now she would keep hers, although she wanted very much to make a pert retort. After all, she knew now that he had lost his wife and probably because of that worked too hard, got too tired and became snappy.

She made her farewells without fuss, gave Podge a final hug and got into the car. She turned to wave as Mr van Tecqx drove away and then sat, her hands clasped on her lap, waiting for him to say something if he felt like it. For her part, she wished very much to jump out of the car and run back home—a childish impulse she instantly suppressed.

She was rewarded by his quiet, 'Your father is a splendid patient. His recovery has surprised me. If he continues to do well, I shall be able to bring forward his second operation by a week at least.'

'At the same hospital? You will have the time? I mean, you live at Delft and I suppose you do most of your work there?'

'I don't work in Delft; I have beds in the hospitals round and about. Leiden—I have consulting rooms there, Rotterdam, Amsterdam and den Haag, and I visit other countries fairly frequently.'

The impatience in his voice stopped her asking any more questions. She knew him well enough by now to know that she would be told anything she needed to know. She relapsed into silence and occupied herself in guessing about the future.

There was a good deal of traffic, especially going through the Dartford Tunnel; it thinned as they drove through Brentwood and on to Harlow and joined the motorway to Bishop's Stortford, where they took the road to Braintree and there, rather to her surprise, stopped outside the White Hart.

'I thought we might have dinner here. The restaurant on board the ferry is often crowded. You will be glad to go straight to your cabin, we dock soon after six o'clock in the morning.'

Emily agreed meekly and got out of the car, and was surprised again to find him at her elbow to shut the door and take her arm as they crossed the pavement.

The meal was well cooked and nicely served, and Emily discovered that she was hungry. They didn't talk much and then on ordinary topics—the weather, the ferries, the state of the roads. Emily tried once or twice to lead their conversations into more personal channels, but Mr van Tecqx was too good for her, he turned a deaf ear and made bland observations on the wet autumn.

The ferry, when they got aboard, was also very full, and she was glad to go to her cabin after all, especially as Mr van Tecqx had sent the stewardess to her with a tray of tea and the information that she would be called at six o'clock and if she needed anything she had only to ring.

There was nothing else to do but to go to bed, and indeed she was tired, although she would have liked to have gone on deck and watched as the ferry left Harwich. She got into her comfortable bunk and, sensible girl that she was, closed her eyes on the doubtful future and slept at once.

It was raining when she left her cabin, carrying her overnight bag, intent on finding Mr van Tecqx. He was outside her cabin door. He took her bag from her, wished her good morning, hoped that she had slept well and suggested that she might like to go on deck as they were almost at the Hoek of Holland.

There was plenty to see, and Emily, careless of the rain, hung over the rails, trying to see everything at once. Unlike most girls of her age, she had had very little chance to travel—France, years ago with her parents, but since then holidays had been few and far between. Mr van Tecqx, standing beside her, studied her intent face under its sensible woolly cap. She looked a good deal younger then her years, partly due to her eagerness and partly due to her unfashionable clothes. All the same, when she turned to say something to him, he had to admit that her eyes were very beautiful; they cancelled out everything else.

Emily gave him an enquiring look and put a hand up to her hair, he was studying her so intently, but then he smiled and she forgot about her hair. Her friends at Pearson's would die if they could see her now, standing with Mr van Tecqx, looking as faultlessly turned out as though he was about to do a ward round. And it wasn't just his clothes, he looked distinguished and completely at ease, and she fancied he was always like that whatever the circumstances; a self-control which made him difficult to know.

He was still watching her, not smiling now, and she said awkwardly, 'I'm sorry, I didn't mean to stare, I was thinking about some of my friends at Pearson's—they'd give anything to be in my shoes, working for you...'

She went slowly red under his raised eyebrows and thinned mouth, and turned away quickly before he should speak. But when he did a few seconds later it was to point out the flat coastline just becoming visible in the dark morning. It spread away from the lights of the harbour, disappearing into a grey nothingness.

'Den Haag is only a few miles along the coast. Delft lies inland, about the same distance away, so we shall be home in good time for breakfast.'

His voice was reassuringly bland, so that her hot cheeks cooled and she was able to make some sort of reply in her quiet voice.

Half an hour later they were driving through the still quiet town. The rain had turned to a steady drizzle, dimming the street lights so that there was little to see. A few miles further on they left the main road and took a side road and Mr van Tecqx said, 'If you look straight ahead you will see Delft.' Sure enough, deceptively near because of the flatness of the land, Emily could see its churches and towers outlined against the fairly grey sky. A little shiver of excitement went through her. Very soon now she would meet her patient. A sudden thought made her ask, 'Does your sister live with you?'

'Since her illness, yes. Normally she lives with my mother in a village a few miles from Delft.'

He said no more than that, leaving her with a head full of questions which she didn't like to ask. But she forgot them as they crossed over the motorway between Rotterdam and den Haag and entered the town.

Its outskirts were modern, well-laid-out, spacious streets with blocks of flats and small neat villas lining them—not at all what Emily had expected, but Mr van Tecqx followed a canal running beside the road and in moments they were in the town's heart. Before her she could see the towering spires of several churches and without thinking she said, 'Oh, look!'

'The Oude Kerk,' explained her companion, 'and the Nieuwe Kerk—that's the one with the very tall spire. The Town Hall is opposite across the Market Square. Delft is quite small—that is, the old town. There are any number of canals and bridges, but it's very easy to explore.'

They crossed one of the narrow hump-backed bridges as he spoke and turned into a narrow street facing yet another canal, with trees, bare now, on either side of it. Along one side of the street were tall, massive houses, red brick with ornate front doors enriched by elaborate plasterwork, their tall wide windows, their small panes gleaming in defiance of the gloomy morning. They stopped half-way down the short street before a house with a rococo façade, its windows in orderly rows on either side of the door.

'Here we are.' Emily could hear the warmth of his voice as he got out and opened her door, crossed the narrow pavement and mounted the three steps to the front door. It was opened as they reached it by a small frail old man who didn't look as though he would have had the strength to budge the heavy carved door. Mr van Tecqx greeted him in his own language before taking Emily's arm. 'This is Bas; he looked after my mother and father, and now he looks after me.'

Emily shook hands and said, 'How do you do?' because she didn't know what else to say, and Bas smiled gently and bowed his head gravely.

'Bas doesn't speak English, but my housekeeper, who is his daughter, has rather more than a smattering. Here she is.'

They had gone from a small lobby into a square hall with doors in either side and an oak staircase with carved banisters facing the door. Emily hadn't expected anything like it: a fair-sized, comfortable house, she had supposed, since Mr van Tecqx seemed prosperous enough, but this house was old and splendid. There were paintings on the panelled walls and a chandelier with sparkling drops, and the room she glimpsed as Bas opened its double doors almost took her breath.

It faced the street, its two large windows taking up almost all of that wall, its lofty ceiling a splendid example of strapwork. It was furnished with a pleasing mixture of comfortable chairs and sofas, lamp tables, and taking up the whole of one wall, a William and Mary cabinet displaying a vast collection of china.

Emily could have stood and gasped and gaped if she had been given the chance, but Mr van Tecqx had thrown his coat down on one of the sofas in what she considered to be a very careless manner and taken up his stance before the brightly burning fire in the big hooded hearth. It was obvious that he was home and pleased to be there.

After a moment he crossed the room to her. 'Let me have that coat. We will have coffee before Anneke takes you to your room. Then if you will come back here I will introduce you to my sister before breakfast.'

He tossed her coat beside his and pulled forward a small armchair. 'Did I tell you her name? I didn't— Lucillia; English is her second language, you will have no difficulty there. When you have met her, I will give you her case history, but I should like you to draw your own conclusions first. Ah, here is coffee. Will you pour?'

Emily thought of the thick mugs of coffee he had been offered at her home as she lifted the silver coffee pot to fill the delicate china cups. She said thoughtfully, 'It was kind of you—I mean, when I gave you coffee at home in a cheap pottery mug...'

He understood her. 'You make excellent coffee,' he said kindly, 'and it never crossed my mind! Have one of these little biscuits. Anneke is proud of her cooking, they are called *sprits*.'

He rambled on, quietly putting her at her ease, so that presently when the door opened and a stout woman of forty or so came in, Emily was able to shake hands with her usual calm manner. She supposed she would see a good deal of Anneke, and it was a relief to find her a cheerful, smiling person, delighted to air her English, and obviously anxious to make her welcome.

They went upstairs together and she showed Emily into a room on one side of the gallery which encircled the hall. It was a very pretty room, furnished in a golden mahogany, the one window curtained in a pale pink damask which matched the bedspread. The carpet was a deeper pink and there were flowers on the little dressing table. Anneke went past her and opened a door to reveal a bathroom, nodding and smiling as she did so. 'Juffrouw Lucillia is there.' She pointed to a door on the other side of the bathroom. 'You come down soon, yes?'

Emily nodded, and as soon as she was alone made a hasty tour of the room. It was charming, and the bathroom held everything a girl could possibly want. She washed her face and hands, put on powder and lipstick, brushed her hair smooth and went back downstairs to where Mr van Tecqx waited for her. His gaze swept over her and he sighed gently. Emily looked half her age and far too meek, and yet when he had first met her he had known that she was right for Lucillia, there was something about her... He shrugged his shoulders.

'Shall we go up, then? I have to go out presently and perhaps that will give you time to get acquainted.'

Emily didn't answer but walked across the hall with him and up the stairs once more, and this time he turned down a short passage leading from the gallery and knocked on the door at its end, at the same time giving Emily an encouraging push as he opened it. His large hand on the small of her back was comforting and re-assuring; she needed both at that moment.

CHAPTER FOUR

IT WAS a large room with two tall windows opening on to a balcony overlooking the surprisingly large garden behind the house. The carpet under Emily's feet was thick and soft and the furniture was almost fragile—Regency mahogany, beautifully inlaid. There was a chaise-longue by the windows and comfortable chairs with circular lamp tables placed in exactly the right places.

Emily took it all in while she stood for a few seconds just inside the door until Mr van Tecqx's hand firmly urged her forward towards the bed. Its occupant was having her breakfast, a bedtable across her knees, but she made to push it away when she saw them.

'Sebastian—oh, you're here at last!' She switched to Dutch, her face alight with pleasure. Such a pretty face too, a feminine version of her brother's with bright blue eyes and fair hair, only her hair curled on her shoulders and her mouth, a softer version than his, drooped at its corners.

Mr van Tecqx sat down on her bed and put an arm around her shoulders. 'I did say I would come,' he observed reasonably, 'and I've brought Emily with me; someone your own age—you can laugh and gossip together until you are well again. How are the legs?'

His sister shrugged her shoulders. 'Oh, all right, I suppose...'

Obedient to a look from Mr van Tecqx, Emily advanced to the bed. She said politely, 'How do you do? It must be very boring for you, getting well again. It would be nice if you were able to dance at Christmas...'

She held out a small capable hand and Lucillia took it reluctantly.

'Oh, that's impossible, I get so tired.' She studied Emily's quiet face. 'You look nice. I dare say we shall get along well enough.'

'I dare say we shall,' agreed Emily cheerfully. 'You must tell me exactly what you can do. I'll come back presently, shall I? When you've had your breakfast.'

She didn't look at Mr van Tecqx but smiled at her patient and slipped out of the room with the speed and quiet of a mouse.

Lucillia looked at her brother. 'She is very plain, but I like her voice.'

'I thought you would. She is like that all the time. I dare say she can get into a towering rage like all women, but I haven't encountered it so far. She isn't much older than you, *liefje*, but I want you to do what she says. I know how boring it is getting well again, and very likely she will take some of that boredom away. I for one will be delighted if you dance, even for a couple of minutes, at Christmas.'

They were speaking in Dutch now and he asked, 'Have you seen Mama lately?'

'Yesterday. She hopes you will go and see her before you go back to England. How long are you staying?'

'I've several cases to see and an outpatients' clinic tomorrow in Leiden—four or five days, I expect.'

Lucillia nibbled at a croissant. 'Have you met any beautiful girls in London?'

'Several.' He smiled at her, but she knew him well enough not to ask any more questions. She said flippantly, 'Well, remember I want to be a bridesmaid at the wedding.'

'Then you had better work hard at your physio.' He got up off the bed and wandered to the door. 'We are going to have breakfast. Emily will be back in a little while.'

Emily was downstairs, doing a round of the portraits in the drawing-room. She had not known where to go and she hadn't liked to look in any of the rooms leading from the hall. The house was very quiet save for a subdued clatter of pans from behind the baize door at the side of the staircase. Perhaps she should have stayed in her room.

She turned from admiring a family group, circa 1820 or so, and saw Mr van Tecqx watching her from the door. 'Breakfast?' he asked mildly.

She went with him very willingly. Her insides were rumbling in a hollow manner, and breakfast was most welcome. Not quite what she had expected, though: a basket of rolls and croissants, toast, a dish of cheese and another of thinly sliced ham, and a stand of boiled eggs, arranged with great elegance on a round table drawn up to the open fire in a small room on the other side of the hall. It was a pretty room, cosily furnished, the wall sconces defeating the grey morning outside, their gentle glow highlighting the silver coffee pot on the table.

Emily, invited to sit down, did so, her small nose wrinkling with pleasure at the aroma from the coffee pot.

'You must be hungry,' observed Mr van Tecqx with detached kindness.

'Well, yes, I am,' she smiled across the table. 'I expect you are, too. While we're eating, will you tell me about your sister? Her treatment and so on?' She took a piece of toast and buttered it. 'She's very pretty—how very hard it must have been for her. There's no reason why she shouldn't get quite well, is there?'

'None at all. She's bored and won't try very hard at the moment. That will be your job, to keep her nose to the grindstone, as it were. She may possibly be left with a very slight limp, but she's not to be told that at present. She has a good deal of movement, but she's lazy about her exercises—the physiotherapist comes each day, but I think that once you have settled in I shall cut her visits down—Lucillia doesn't like her and I suspect that she doesn't like Lucillia, who can be very tiresome. She may do more for you. She becomes very impatient with her crutches and loses heart easily.' He passed his cup for more coffee. 'You see, Emily, your side of the bargain is to be a hard one.'

'I'll do my best.'

'I know that, otherwise would I have asked you to take on the job?'

Bas came in with fresh coffee and Mr van Tecqx said, 'I shall drive over to see my mother after I have seen my patients. Ask for anything you may need, Anneke will give you all the help you need, and Bas will look after you. We will discuss your free time when I get back. The physiotherapist comes at eleven o'clock. Be there and watch what she does. There is no reason why you shouldn't take over the simple exercises. If you have finished . . . ?'

Emily had been thrown in at the deep end, and perhaps that was a good idea. The sooner she got to know her patient the better, and it was evident that Mr van Tecqx intended her to find out things for herself. Well, she would. She rose from the table, murmured suitably and went up to her room, where she had a shower, changed into one of the overalls and went along to Lucillia's room.

The voice that answered her knock was cross, and she found Lucillia lounging in bed, staring at the ceiling.

'Hello,' said Emily. 'Could you be bothered to tell me about your day? Do you get up before the physiotherapist comes?'

'I get up if I feel like it.' Lucillia sounded sulky. 'I don't feel like it!'

'Too bad,' observed Emily briskly. 'I haven't a clue where everything is, I shall get lost in this house if you don't help and I can't speak a word of Dutch. I was counting on getting you into your chair and pushing you around to show me everything.'

'Sebastian should have done that—or told Anneke...'

'I dare say he was too busy to think about that.' Emily strolled to the window. 'Oh, well, I'll go and unpack. I don't suppose anyone will mind if I explore on my own?'

'I can't go anywhere except on this floor,' grumbled Lucillia.

'True. Though I expect when your brother comes home he might carry you downstairs—your chair folds up, doesn't it? I can carry it down and we could whisk round the ground floor—if it would only stop raining we might go out into the garden too. I don't suppose you've tried to walk?' Emily put the question idly.

'Oh, once or twice, but it's such a bother—those silly crutches!' Lucillia still sounded cross, but she had pulled herself up in the bed and was looking at Emily. 'Tell me about yourself. When I spoke to Sebastian and asked

him about you, he said it was difficult to describe you—
I can't think why.'

Emily came back from the window and sat down on
the bed. 'Well, I can,' she said sensibly. 'I don't suppose
he's really looked at me. I mean, I'm hardly a raving
beauty, am I?'

Lucillia laughed. 'You know, I think I'm going to like
you, Emily. I might even do some of the things you want
me to do. Now tell me about yourself.'

So Emily told, being deliberately light-hearted about
it, describing Podge, even making a joke of her room
at Mrs Winter's.

'Just one room?' asked Lucillia, in horror. 'But you
can't live and sleep in one poky room!'

'Lots of people do. Now tell me, who has been looking
after you? Someone must have bathed you and got you
in and out of bed...'

'Zuster Brugge—she left yesterday evening. Anneke
saw to me this morning. I hated Zuster Brugge, she had
hard hands and she was always telling me about the
patients in hospital who had to do what they were told
and no nonsense.' Lucillia looked at Emily. 'Do you
think I am spoiled?'

Emily laughed. 'Oh, yes,' she said comfortably, 'but
I shan't hold that against you. The physiotherapist comes
soon, doesn't she? May I stay and watch? Your brother
thought that perhaps she need not come quite so often
if I could learn the exercises you need to do.' She got
off the bed. 'I'll get a bowl and you can wash your face
and hands and do your face, and when she's finished,
we'll see about getting you under the shower.'

'Zuster Brugge said I couldn't have a shower until I
learnt to help myself.'

'Well, let's make her eat her words!'

Lucillia bore the physiotherapist's treatment very badly; she complained that she was being hurt, that it was all useless, anyway, and that she was going to die. Emily, listening soberly, sighed inwardly. Mr van Tecqx had spoken nothing but the truth. His sister was going to be a handful.

The physiotherapist went, and they had coffee and talked about clothes.

'Do you love pretty things?' asked Lucillia, looking pointedly at Emily's serviceable and severe overall. She sounded surprised.

'Very much—there's not much chance to wear them and dress up when you're a nurse.' Emily put down her cup. 'Now for that shower before lunch.'

It was an awkward business. Lucillia had still very limited movement in her legs. Emily eased her into her chair and wheeled it to the bathroom leading from the room, and turned on the shower. It was specially built with a little seat under it, and after a good deal of manoeuvring and giggling on both their parts, Lucillia was safely under it, while Emily, wrapped in a pinny she found hanging behind the door, sponged and rubbed and shampooed. They emerged some time later, rather damp and flushed but still good friends.

'You see,' said Emily in her sensible voice, 'it can be done—I know it's a struggle, but it's worth it.'

She applied herself to drying her patient's hair and offered her her make-up box, and Lucillia, in a pretty dressing-gown and once more back in her chair, had to admit that she felt a good deal better. 'Although it's a frightful fuss and bother,' she complained.

Emily thought it prudent to say nothing. She went in search of Bas, who led her to the kitchen where Anneke was hovering over lunch trays.

'You must ring for anything you want, miss,' she said. 'One of the maids will bring up Juffrouw Lucillia's meal. You have your meal in the small room?'

However, when Emily went back to make sure that Lucillia had all she wanted she was told to have her lunch with her. 'I like to hear you talk.' Lucillia spoke to the maid and presently a second tray was brought and laid on a small table by Emily's chair.

They were deep in discussion on the latest skirt length when the door opened and Mr van Tecqx came in.

He wasn't alone. A St Bernard stalked beside him and darting ahead of them, barking with delight, was a Jack Russell.

Lucillia gave a happy little scream. 'Sidney, Pepper, darlings—Sebastian, may they stay? I thought you were having lunch with Mama?'

He crossed the room and sat down on the edge of the bed. 'Yes, they may stay if Emily has no objection.' He glanced at her briefly. 'The former nurse had a horror of dogs. I had lunch with Mama,' he glanced at his watch, 'an hour ago—it's after half past one.'

There was a faint question in his voice. It seemed prudent to explain.

'Well,' began Emily, 'we got a bit carried away. Lucillia had a shower and I washed her hair—she's going back to bed as soon as we've finished lunch. You don't mind?'

'I'm delighted. How did the physio go?'

'Oh, I was good, wasn't I, Emily?' Lucillia didn't wait for an answer. 'Sebastian darling, how soon can I go shopping? I need some new clothes, I mean once I'm walking again—I managed on my crutches...' She turned her pretty face to his. 'Dear Sebastian!'

He got up and strolled over to the window and looked out at his garden below. 'Don't let us rush things—the moment you can walk round the garden on your crutches you may have an entire new wardrobe. But don't run before you can walk, *liefje*—and I warn you, there will be days when you will feel that you will never walk again, even though you'll dance at my wedding one day.'

A remark which sent an unhappy little pang through Emily, although she wasn't sure why. Sidney was standing beside her chair and she pulled his soft ears gently and didn't look up, but Lucillia gave a squeal of laughter.

'Sebastian, you're never going to marry? Who is she?'

'I'll have to find her before you start dancing, won't I?' he said blandly, and Emily gave a sigh of relief. Lucillia had been ill for ten months now. She thought it would take at least another two months before she would be free of her crutches. Her left leg had been the most affected and the muscle wastage was considerable. She gave a little gasp at her thoughts; she had come to nurse Lucillia back to health as soon as possible and then go back to England; that had been the bargain, and here she was hoping she would be in this lovely old house for months. She went a bright pink with shame and Mr van Tecqx, watching her downbent head, wondered why.

'If you've finished that soufflé I'll lift you into bed,' and he suited the action to the word. 'You can have a nap while Emily unpacks and finds her way around.' He kissed the top of Lucillia's head and went to the door. 'Emily, I'll ask Anneke to take you round the house. I shall be back late this evening.'

With Lucillia tucked up in bed with a book, Emily
went to her room, unpacked her case, tidied herself and
went downstairs, not quite sure what to do next. Bas was
in the hall, waiting for her. He beamed at her without
speaking and led her through the baize door to where
Anneke was waiting in a comfortable sitting room. She
surged up as Emily went in, smiling as widely as her
father. 'I am to show you all,' she explained. 'We start
here. Our sitting-room—there are four of us, and here
the kitchen.'

It was a delightfully old-fashioned room with its
scrubbed table in the centre, rows of copper pans and
saucepans, a dresser loaded with dishes and plates and,
looking not in the least out of place, a big Aga stove
before which sat a tabby cat. 'Nice?' asked Anneke.

'Oh, lovely.' Emily went slowly round, admiring
everything, then stood at the lattice windows overlooking the garden at the back of the house.

'And here...' Anneke led the way through a stout door
to a narrow passage with several small rooms leading
from it. There were modern sinks and fridges and deep-
freezes, a dishwasher and an ironing-room, all very
modern and kept nicely out of sight.

They went back through the kitchen and out into the
hall, where Anneke opened doors into the drawing-room,
the dining-room, and a small sitting-room furnished exquisitely in Regency style and where Emily thought she
could spend the rest of her days very happily, it was so
pretty.

There was a vast library with a gallery running round
three of the walls and leather chairs disposed around the
parquet floor, each with its own small table and lamp,
and a billiard room across the hall. The last door opened

on to Mr van Tecqx's study, but Emily didn't go in, only stood at the doorway and looked at the great desk and chair behind it. Here, presumably, he retired when he wanted peace and quiet. The top of the desk was very untidy and the waste-paper basket beside it was brimming over. Emily, having a tidy mind, itched to empty it and restore order to the chaos.

Upstairs there were a bewildering number of bedrooms, all looking as though they were in use, and when Emily remarked on that, Anneke said, 'It is that Mijnheer wishes that the house is kept open, you understand?'

She led the way to the second floor, where there were more rooms, each charmingly furnished, most with bathrooms. The upkeep! thought Emily, a bit dazed with such lavish comfort, and followed her guide up still another staircase, narrow and steep, where the attic rooms house a flat for Anneke and Bas and the two housemaids. There was comfort here too; a small kitchen, a sitting-room and two shower-rooms.

She accompanied Anneke down to the hall once more and once there, ventured, 'It's a very large house just for Mr van Tecqx.'

'Yes, yes, very large. But always his family is living here with many children. He has a brother and sisters, there were six children. When Mijnheer married we hoped for children again...' She shook her head sadly and Emily, dying of curiosity, took her tongue between her teeth; it was none of her business.

Lucillia was awake when she went along to her room and inclined to be peevish, but she soon cheered up over tea and biscuits and submitted cheerfully to Emily's ministrations, and when they were done, the pair of them watched a programme on television. It was a splendid set with remote control, and when Lucillia switched to the BBC news, Emily had a sudden pang of homesickness. Pearson's would be busy at this hour; she pictured the ward and Sister Cook sailing up and down, keeping an eagle eye on everything. Her thoughts were diverted by Lucillia's sudden, 'Have you ever been in love, Emily?'

'Well, no,' said Emily slowly. 'I've never got to know a man well enough.'

Lucillia looked astonished. 'You didn't go out dancing or dining? All those young doctors...'

Emily said in a matter-of-fact voice, 'Yes, I know, but I'm not pretty and not chatty, if you see what I mean. I don't sparkle.'

Lucillia nodded her pretty head. 'Oh, yes, I see, but you are nice to be with, Emily. I'm glad Sebastian found you. He didn't like Zuster Brugge: he said he was frightened of her—he wasn't really, of course, he said that to make me laugh.' She switched off the television. 'Emily, do you truly believe that I'll be quite normal again?'

'Yes, I do. Look what you've done today. We'll do the same tomorrow and the day after that, and each week we'll do a little bit more. You are going to dance again, you know.'

'At Sebastian's wedding—his wife died years ago and he's never bothered to marry again. He has lots of friends, of course, but that's not the same as getting married, is it? Besides, they are all married people. Every so often they introduce him to some girl or other that they think might be suitable, but he doesn't fall in love.'

'Oh, well, he will, one day,' Emily observed in her sensible way. It would be someone suitable—it would have to be, with this lovely house to preside over. Dinner parties, thought Emily, seeing it all clearly in her mind's eye, and people dropping in for lunch and tennis in the summer...

'What are you thinking about?' asked Lucillia.

'Nothing. How about a few passive movements before your dinner?'

Emily discovered that she was to have her own dinner downstairs after she had seen to Lucillia, and it was almost eight o'clock before her patient had finished the dainty meal which had been sent up for her and had been settled with a pile of magazines. 'Zuster Brugge made me go to sleep at nine o'clock, she said it was good for me. You won't, will you, Emily?'

'Only if Mr van Tecqx wants you to. Are you quite comfy?'

She went to her room and debated as to whether she should put on a dress, and decided that she would. There was nothing much more to do for Lucillia and she could put on the pinny in the bathroom. She did her face and brushed out her hair and tied it back, then got into the other dress, apart from the navy blue, that she had bought at C & A during their last sale. It was what a woman's magazine would have described as useful, for although it was nicely cut it had no high fashion points and was in a serviceable grey jersey.

Emily, examining herself in the long looking-glass inside the big closet door, felt instantly dissatisfied, and then laughed at her reflection. There was no one to see her anyway.

In this she was mistaken. Mr van Tecqx rose from his chair as she entered the drawing-room on Bas's invitation. He said easily, 'Hullo—I thought we might dine together, we can discuss Lucillia. She's not asleep yet? I'll have a chat with her later.'

'She's reading and watching television; she's tired, I think, but quite happy too.'

She sat down in the chair he had pulled forward and accepted the glass of sherry he had fetched for her, uneasily aware that her appearance hardly did justice to her splendid surroundings. Her host didn't appear to notice that; he chatted about various things and asked her if she had seen the house and if she had liked it, and mentioned that he would be going back to England in a few days' time. 'I'll look your father up,' he promised. 'You have telephoned him?'

'Me?' She was surprised. 'No.'

He stretched over and picked up the telephone which was lying on a small table near him. 'What is your number, Emily?' When he had got it he asked, 'Would you like me to go?'

'No, thank you. If I just tell Father that I'm here...'

She made the call brief and hung up. 'Father's feeling fine; he walked down to the gate and back several times.'

'Good. What do you think of Lucillia?'

There was a picture of her over the great fireplace, and Emily studied it. 'She's so pretty.' She sighed unconsciously. 'And she does want to be quite well again, despite what she sometimes says, doesn't she? I think I can understand why she's so impatient. She's missing so much.'

'Have you not missed a great deal too, Emily?' He spoke very softly and didn't look at her, so that she was emboldened to go on.

'Well, yes, I suppose you could say that, but I never expected anything else.' She added quickly, in case he thought she was sorry for herself, 'You can't compare us, you know.'

'Comparisons are odious,' declared Mr van Tecqx, getting up to let the two dogs in. Back in his chair with the two of them on either side of him, he observed, 'I have left you to get on with things today; you seem to have managed very well. Tomorrow we must put our heads together and get some sort of scheme organised. You must, of course, have your free time, and a day to yourself each week. There is a car in the garage, and the gardener will drive you anywhere you may wish to go.'

'Thank you. I expect I'll spend the first few weeks getting to know Delft.'

'Just as you please.' He was politely uninterested, and Emily sat trying to think of something amusing or interesting to say without success until Bas appeared to tell them that dinner was served, and that was a great relief.

Emily was too sensible to be overawed by the richness of the silver and crystal with which the table was decked. All the same, she made a mental note of it all so that she could write about it later to her friends at Pearson's and her father. She ate her mushrooms *au gratin*, Dover sole in a white wine sauce, accompanied by creamed potatoes and a variety of vegetables, and polished off a strawberry mousse topped with lashings of whipped cream with the delicacy of a kitten enjoying a saucer of milk. She accepted a glass of wine when Mr van Tecqx offered it, but refused a second glass; she still had to settle her patient for the night.

Mindful of her manners, she made polite conversation throughout the meal, encouraged by her companion's apparent interest in such mundane topics as the weather, Dutch architecture and gardening. Indeed, he led her to suppose she had brushed through the meal rather well, so she was a little puzzled when he asked her as she poured their coffee, 'Emily, when was the last time you went out with a man? I know you have been out with me, but other than that?'

She put down the coffee-pot carefully and handed him his cup. 'Well, I think it was about a year ago. Roseanne—she's one of my friends at Pearson's—her brother came to take her out one evening, but she'd already promised to go out with one of the housemen, so I went instead of her because he'd booked a table at a Chinese restaurant and he didn't want to go alone. I don't think I like Chinese food.'

Mr van Tecqx allowed a small choking sound to escape his lips. 'Er—no, it isn't to everyone's taste.'

'Why did you ask?'

'No reason,' his voice was bland, 'idle curiosity. You must forgive me. I know so little about you.'

That goes for the two of us, thought Emily as she offered more coffee.

He left her presently, sitting comfortably in the drawing-room while he went to say goodnight to his sister. The house was quiet, but not unpleasantly so. The *stoelklok* on the wall tick-tocked as it must have done for very many years, and there were faint sounds from the dining-room where one of the maids was clearing the table. Outside there was the muted sound of traffic at the end of the street. Emily sighed blissfully. It was all quite perfect.

She said goodnight to Mr van Tecqx when he came back, and he made no move to detain her. His 'See you in the morning, Emily,' was uttered in a voice that led her to suppose he was thinking about something else.

She settled Lucillia for the night and went to her own bed. It had been a long day and she was tired. Just before she went to sleep she decided that Mr van Tecqx had been mistaken about his sister; she wasn't going to be difficult.

Emily was forced to eat her words before the next day was over. Lucillia began the day well enough, but when there was some difficulty in getting her physio exercises right she burst into tears and grew so wild that the physiotherapist went away, saying her services were useless for the moment, which left Emily to bear the full force of Lucillia's rage.

'It's not fair!' she wept. 'Why should someone like you be on your feet and perfectly well—you don't need to be, you don't go dancing or to parties, I'm sure you are not that kind of girl, but I am—I won't, simply won't lie here day in and day out!' and when Emily fetched a bowl and started to sponge her face, she screamed, 'Oh, go away, do! I want to die!'

Emily took no notice. This was what Mr van Tecqx had warned her of. Well, it couldn't last for ever. She mopped her patient's tear-stained face, shook up the pillows and got everything ready for the shower.

'I won't!' shouted Lucillia. 'And you can't make me! Where is Sebastian?'

'I haven't seen him this morning.' Emily kept her voice calm. 'I dare say he has patients to see. But you don't want him to see you like this, do you?'

'Why not? It won't be the first time.' Lucillia burst into tears again and caught Emily's hand. 'Oh, I'm a beast, aren't I? Don't go away, will you, Emily? If you knew how desperate I feel!'

Emily perched on the bed and took Lucillia into her arms. 'I can't know exactly, but I think it must be pretty grim. But you're over the worst; if only you'd believe that! Getting better is always worse than being ill, because when you're ill you don't care, but once you know you're on the mend you get impatient.' She patted Lucillia's hand and her silk-clad shoulder. 'I'll help you all I can.'

Lucillia went on crying, but the rage had gone out of her now. Emily was still sitting there when Mr van Tecqx opened the door and came in. Sidney and Pepper were with him, but at his quiet word they sat down obediently just inside the door and they didn't bark.

'I met Juffrouw Smit,' he remarked placidly. 'She wrung her hands at me and said she couldn't cope. She was wild-eyed. Did you threaten the poor woman with murder?'

Lucillia gave a watery giggle into Emily's shoulder and then lifted her head. 'Oh, Sebastian, must she come back? She is so bossy, and she makes me do things which hurt.'

'Oh, yes, she's coming back, and you'll do as you are told, *liefje*, just to please Mama and the family and me. Did you threaten Emily as well?'

Lucillia nodded. 'Yes, but I didn't mean it, did I, Emily?'

'Of course not.' Emily stood up and smoothed her crumpled overall and tucked a strand of mousy hair behind an ear, and Mr van Tecqx looked at her thoughtfully. She looked rather the worse for wear, but she was still calm. 'Have you come to visit?' she asked. 'I'll go and fetch the coffee, shall I?'

'Bas is bringing it up, we'll have that together and then you can dump Lucillia under the shower.' He took no heed of his sister's rebellious look but made himself comfortable on the window seat, where he stayed drinking his coffee and talking unconcernedly about nothing in particular. By the time they had finished Lucillia was in a better frame of mind and agreed rather grumpily to having a shower, whereupon her brother picked her up out of bed and set her on her chair, wheeled her into the bathroom and then wandered off, leaving Emily to get on with it.

Although Lucillia had calmed down, done her exercises, and sat obediently in her chair for a good deal of the day, even walked, with Emily's help, a few steps with her crutches, Emily, tucking her patient up for the night, felt that very little progress had been made. She had dined alone with Bas hovering over her, making sure she ate the delicious food Anneke had prepared for her, and now, with Lucillia quiet now and settled for the night, she was free to go to her room and go to bed herself. Although she was tired, she wasn't sleepy; she would have enjoyed a brisk walk in the fresh air, only that was hardly possible on a dark November night. She went to the window and drew aside the curtains and looked out on to the dark. Mr van Tecqx had said she would have to take the rough with the smooth, and certainly today had been rough.

A tap on the door roused her and when she called come in Anneke put her head round it. 'If you will go to the study?' she asked. 'Mijnheer wishes you there.'

Emily had kicked off her shoes. She put them back on and followed the housekeeper downstairs. Mr van Tecqx had remembered her free time, she thought hopefully, or what was more likely, he had some instructions about his sister.

Neither. He got up from his desk as she went in and waved her to a chair. 'You are not tired?' His tone implied that she had better not be. 'Good—I'll run you over to my mother's house; she is anxious to meet you, and a change of scene will do you good.'

'Lucillia?' began Emily.

'Anneke will keep an eye on her. Get your coat, will you, and we will be off.'

It was hardly an invitation, more a command. She got to her feet again and went through the door he was holding open for her, and was completely taken by surprise when he stooped and kissed her cheek as she went past him.

'Well, I never,' muttered Emily as she went on her way in search of her coat. 'That's twice!'

CHAPTER FIVE

IT WAS all very well for Mr van Tecqx to tell her to get her coat in an offhand fashion. Emily took off her overall, spent a few minutes over her face and hair, changed her shoes, and only then got her coat from the closet and put it on. Staring at her reflection, she concluded that she looked exactly how she felt—tired and plain and dressed quite unsuitably. Men, thought Emily bitterly, and Mr van Tecqx in particular, could be very tiresome.

He was waiting in the hall leaning up against a wall, talking to Bas, but as she joined them he clapped the old man on the shoulders and urged her through the door, then got into the car without speaking. It seemed rather late in the day to pay a visit, but to let him know this seemed a useless exercise; Mr van Tecqx had demonstrated enough during the last few weeks that if he had made up his mind he wasn't to be budged.

He drove through the lighted streets in the direction of den Haag and after only a mile or so turned down a narrow unlighted lane. Emily couldn't see anything much in the dark. The car's lights showed a narrow canal on one side of the road and fields beyond and, as far as she could make out, fields on the other side too. There were no houses, although lights twinkled here and there away from the road. Presently she saw a high wall, brick and well maintained, and ahead of them in the curve of the lane, a pair of wrought iron gates, open.

Mr van Tecqx hadn't spoken; he didn't speak as he drove through the gateway, up a short drive and stopped before a well lighted house. He got out, opened her door and took her arm to cross the sweep to a solid front door with a handsome portico, well lighted. As they reached it it was opened by a stout elderly woman who beamed at them both and addressed herself to Mr van Tecqx, which gave Emily a chance to glance around her. The house was of brick like the wall, with a flat front and windows on either side of the door. Not over-large, but she had the impression of age and solidarity and perfect quiet. Luxury too, she added silently as she went inside.

The vestibule led into a large hall, much larger than that in the house in Delft, and the staircase rose from its centre and branched left and right to the gallery above. The ceiling was high and ornate, but there was no chandelier, only sconces between the panelled walls, casting a glow over the carpet underfoot and the heavy, carved oak table, bare save for a centrepiece of chrysanthemums. There were several doors leading from the hall. The stout woman went ahead of them and opened double doors at once on one side, saying something to someone in the room as she did so, and Emily, propelled gently forward by Mr van Tecqx, went past her and across what seemed to her nervous mind to be an endless carpet, to fetch up before an elderly lady sitting in a winged chair to one side of the fireplace.

She hadn't, until that moment, had much idea of whom she was to meet, but with hindsight she had expected someone imposing, tall and elegant. She had been wrong to a large extent; the lady she faced was small and not at all imposing. She had a face as lacking in good looks as Emily's own, but her eyes sparkled and her smile was delightful, and when she got to her feet it was somehow comforting to see that she was the same height. The elegance was there, but it was the understated elegance of an older woman who could spend what she wanted on her clothes and knew what suited her.

She offered a cheek to her son and smiled up at him. 'You have brought Emily to see me...' She turned to her and held out a hand. 'I am so sorry to encroach on your evening, but I did want to meet you, and Sebastian is going back to London tomorrow—it seemed a good idea for us to meet before he goes away again.'

Emily said how do you do in her quiet voice and took the chair she was offered. Her relief at finding Mr van Tecqx's mother a perfectly ordinary person like anyone else's mother was so great that she smiled widely, and the colour came back into her cheeks, which had paled with misgiving. Something which Mr van Tecqx noted with interest.

He sat down opposite Emily and his mother ignored him. 'I am so very relieved to have you with us, my dear,' she began in an English as good as Emily's. 'Lucillia has been ill for months now, and somehow she had come to a halt and I felt that she had resigned herself—through boredom, probably—to remaining an invalid. Zuster Brugge was very good, but Lucillia took a dislike to her and instead of making progress she has been going steadily backwards. I was delighted when Sebastian told me that he had found just the person to help us. She is a shockingly bad patient, you know, but I do hope that you will stay and help her to recover. She is the youngest of my children and hopelessly spoilt by all of us.'

A young girl brought in coffee, and Mevrouw van Tecqx poured it and went on, 'Will you mind spending

Christmas with us? My other daughters and their husbands and children will be here...'

She sounded so wistful that Emily said at once, 'I think I shall enjoy it very much, *mevrouw*. And Lucillia is determined to get well—I only hope I'll be able to help her.'

'I am sure that she will get better and that you will be able to help her. She can be very difficult...'

'Well, I dare say we should be that too if we couldn't walk properly,' observed Emily matter-of-factly.

Lucillia's mother nodded. 'I shall come over to see her tomorrow—stay for tea if I may? I have been living in Sebastian's house for a good many months, but this house cannot be left for too long.' She smiled a little. 'I have become a little tired...'

'Of course. It's so much worse when it's someone you love who is ill.'

'Yes, you understand that, don't you, Emily?'

Mevrouw van Tecqx turned to look at her son. 'There is a good deal to see in Delft. Emily will enjoy exploring.'

He answered casually, and presently they got up to go. Bidden a kind goodnight by her hostess, Emily hoped she had passed muster, for that, she had decided, was what the visit had been all about. She sat silently as they drove back to Delft and once in the house bade Mr van Tecqx goodnight.

Half-way up the staircase she was stopped by his, 'I leave for England early tomorrow. Have you any messages for your father? I intend to see him while I'm there.'

'Please tell him I'm very comfortable and happy, and give him my love. I hope you have a good journey, Mr van Tecqx.'

'Thank you. Goodnight.' He turned away to go to his study and Emily went on upstairs, to make sure Lucillia was all right before going to her own room.

The days slid quietly by, some better than others, but Lucillia's progress, although slow and erratic, was getting ahead. Mr van Tecqx telephoned each evening, and her mother visited frequently and one or two of Lucillia's friends came for coffee or tea, and each day Emily battled with the shower, her patient's often expressed wish not to get out of her bed, not to walk, not to do her exercises... It was tiring, sometimes exhausting, and she would have liked a respite, but until Mr van Tecqx got back and made some arrangement regarding her free day, she had no intention of taking one.

It was December now and the weather had turned cold. There was even a hint of snow, and Emily, taking a brisk daily walk round the garden with the dogs, sniffed at the icy air with pleasure. The garden, while not large, was well laid out and the shrubs and trees, thickly frosted, made an excellent background for the old house.

The feast of Sint Nicolaas was only a day or so away. Emily had heard all about it from Lucillia; her sisters and their husbands and children would be spending it with her mother, but of course, they would all come and see her. The Saint and his attendant Zwarte Piet would be arriving in Delft in the afternoon and the children would be taken to see him. 'I expect you'll go with them,' observed Lucillia. 'He is on horseback, you know, and Zwarte Piet walks beside him with his sack and birch broom—it's the greatest fun!'

She sounded so wistful that Emily said instantly, 'It sounds super, but I'd just as soon stay here with you.'

The following day Mr van Tecqx's sisters arrived. They came circumspectly, one at a time with their husbands and children so that Lucillia wouldn't get too tired. Emily met them in turn: Reilike, the eldest, named after a Friesian grandmother, with her husband Sieme and their three children, Ludolf, Tilde and Iwert, the eldest eight years old, the youngest five. They shook hands solemnly with Emily and sat, on their best behaviour, eating biscuits and drinking their lemonade for the half-hour visit. After lunch Jessica and Jan arrived with their twins Jake and Jill, ten years old, brimming over with energy and full of curiosity about Emily. She entertained them while their parents talked to Lucillia, and she was sorry to see them go. It was after tea when the third sister arrived, only a year or two older than Lucillia and very like her in appearance. She had a small baby and a young, pleasant-faced husband called Willem, a simple name in contrast to her own—Theodosia—although Lucillia addressed her as Theo. The baby, still very small, was called Kleine Willem and he slept peacefully throughout the visit.

Lucillia was tired when her last visitor had left. Emily made short work of getting her ready for the night, persuaded her to eat her supper in bed and then, since Lucillia was over-excited and restless, sat herself down close to the bed, with a lamp close at her elbow, and opened *Vanity Fair*, a book Lucillia had wished to read but had thought too difficult.

The characters came alive in Emily's quiet voice, and she had paused to agree with Lucillia that Amelia Osborne was the most tiresome milksop that ever walked when they were joined by Mr van Tecqx.

Lucillia gave a small shriek of delight. 'Sebastian, when did you get back? You'll be here for Sint Nicolaas. Will you be home for a long time? Did you bring me anything from London?'

He bent to kiss her. 'How's my girl? Have the family been to see you? Mama has them all staying, I suppose...' He looked across at Emily. 'Everything is going well?' He sat down on the edge of the bed and Sidney and Pepper arranged themselves at his feet.

'I believe so,' said Emily, and thought how splendid he looked, lounging on the bed, one arm around his sister's shoulders.

'You haven't said,' interpolated Lucillia. 'When did you get home, and for how long?'

'Just a few minutes ago, and for the next few weeks. I had to be here for Sint Nicolaas and I don't expect to go to England until the New Year. Have you had dinner?'

'Yes. I'm a bit tired, so Emily put me to bed and I had it on a tray.'

'And Emily?' He glanced across at her with raised eyebrows.

Lucillia answered for her. 'She was reading to me—to soothe me, you know.'

'Do you feel soothed enough to rest for half an hour while we have dinner? I'm famished, and I dare say Emily is too.'

'Will you come back here?'

'Yes. What is more, you shall have a little package to open while we're away.' He took a small box from a pocket and put it into her hands. 'We'll admire them when we get back. Come, Emily...'

They dined rather grandly, sitting opposite one another at the big table with Bas serving them. Mr van

Tecqx kept up a steady stream of gentle talk about nothing much until they were drinking their coffee.

'I saw your father, Emily. He is making splendid progress, and if the other joint is as successful he will be a new man.'

'I'll never be able to thank you enough, Mr van Tecqx. I do hope Lucillia will be a new girl too.' Emily added a little anxiously, 'She really does try.'

'Yes, I know. If you have finished shall we go upstairs?'

Lucillia was sitting up in bed, looking happy. 'Sebastian, however did you know? Look, Emily—aren't they gorgeous?'

She was wearing the earrings her brother had brought her; big gold hoops dangling on either side of her pretty face. 'They're all the rage!' She asked, 'Do you wear earrings, Emily?'

'Well, no—I'm in uniform for most of the time and they'd look funny.'

'Don't you ever go out? With men, I mean—dancing and so on?'

Mr van Tecqx answered for her. He said smoothly, 'Emily leads far too busy a life until she has finished her training. Did Reilike and Theo come? Did Jessica bring the twins? They will all be here for tea tomorrow. Mama will stay with you while we watch St Nicolaas arrive.'

Lucillia's pretty mouth turned down at the corners. 'I'd like to go...'

'You'll come downstairs for tea with all of us before we open our presents.' He bent and kissed her cheek. 'Sleep well, my dear.'

'You are going out?'

He smiled faintly. 'Yes. Goodnight, Emily.'

When he had gone Emily shook up the pillows and straightened the duvet. Lucillia took off the earrings and put them back in their box. 'Sebastian is such a dear,' she observed. 'I hope he has fun this evening; I expect he is going out with Beatrix van Telle. She's been after him for years, but he says he is too busy to get married. After all, his first wife wasn't much of a success.'

Emily longed to hear more; a well-put question or two and Lucillia might enlarge upon this interesting aspect of her brother's life. With commendable restraint she murmured in a negative fashion and made some harmless remark about the next day's events, and presently tucked her patient up for the night and went to bed herself.

Lucillia was inclined to be peevish in the morning. Emily settled her with her breakfast tray and went down to eat her own meal. The house was quiet, although Bas came to wish her good morning and bring the coffee-pot. There was no sign of the master of the house. Probably in bed still, sleeping it off, decided Emily, buttering a roll and sinking her splendid teeth into it. She wasn't looking forward to the day. She suspected that Lucillia was going to be difficult, and there had been this talk about presents, and even if she had known if she should give them and to whom, she had had no chance to go to the shops. She went back upstairs, re-arranging her features into their normal calm appearance. Which was a good thing, for Lucillia had no wish to do any of the things she was asked to do. The physiotherapist was not coming, so that Emily had the task of putting her through her exercises before getting her under the shower.

She couldn't walk, she declared, she was crippled for life, so what was the point of struggling round with her crutches? 'If I had the strength I would throw them out of the window!' she cried at Emily.

'Well, if you had the strength, you wouldn't need them, so that would be the best place for them,' observed Emily, at her most sensible.

'Where is Sebastian?' demanded Lucillia. 'Why am I left alone just with you? I want him here!'

Emily glanced at her watch. 'It's still quite early; I dare say he's tired after having a long journey yesterday.'

'I don't care!' Lucillia was rapidly working herself into a tantrum.

'Don't care was made to care, don't care was hung, don't care was put in the pot and boiled till he was done,' recited Emily, and shot round at the great laugh from the door.

'I haven't heard that since my old nanny used to scold me,' said Mr van Tecqx. 'And what is all the fuss about? If you don't cheer up, Lucillia, Sint Nicolaas won't come near you. I've come to carry you downstairs, but you are not even dressed.'

Lucillia said sulkily, 'I don't want to go downstairs. I shall stay here in a dressing-gown all day.'

He walked over to the cupboard along one wall and opened its doors. 'Emily, what shall she wear? There was a pretty blue thing—I don't see it.' Not surprising, really, as there were a dozen or more dresses hanging there.

'This one?' asked Emily, and gave a gentle tug to the skirt of a blue wool dress—the blue matched Lucillia's eyes exactly.

He reached up and got the dress and put it on the bed. 'Mama is downstairs, she will lunch with us. Everyone else will come early this afternoon. Don't spoil her day, *liefje.*' His voice was gentle and very kind. 'What is more, you are going to show her how well you can walk. I'll be back in ten minutes.'

It took every second of that time, but Emily managed it. Even the earrings were in place. He glanced at her as he came thoughtfully into the room; her face wore its usual calm expression, but her neat head was untidy and there was a faint flush on her cheeks. She said cheerfully, 'Lucillia is quite ready—don't the earrings look pretty?'

'Very. Lucillia, I want you to walk towards me. You won't fall—if you take six steps you shall have a gold chain to match those earrings.'

It was worth the effort, thought Emily, watching the girl going towards him on her crutches, and beamed with pleasure when she reached him.

'Splendid. If you try really hard, my dear, you will soon be able to manage with one crutch.'

He took them from her and handed them to Emily, picked up his sister and carried her downstairs to where her mother was waiting in the drawing-room. Emily, following after, set the crutches tidily against a wall, wished Mevrouw van Tecqx good morning and felt disappointment when Mr van Tecqx suggested that she might like to have her coffee in peace and quiet. She said, 'Of course,' in her calm voice, and went back upstairs to tidy Lucillia's room before the maid came to make the bed and restore it to its usual pristine state.

Mevrouw van Tecqx had looked surprised, but she had said nothing, only when Anneke brought in the coffee she asked if she would take a tray up to Emily. Only when she had done so did she say, 'You don't mind, Sebastian? The child looked as though she could do with a cup of coffee, and I am sure that she would never ring the bell for anyone to bring it to her.'

He frowned a little. 'I'm sorry, I had no intention of neglecting her.'

'You are satisfied with her work?'

'Indeed I am. Lucillia is making progress, for the simple reason that Emily gives her little chance to do otherwise.' He smiled at his sister. 'You like her, don't you, my dear?'

'Oh, yes. She is never cross and she laughs a lot just as though she's always happy. I quite forget how plain she is.'

'Her eyes are beautiful.' Sebastian put down his coffee cup. 'I will be back directly.'

His mother poured herself another cup of coffee and said nothing to this, but when he had gone she asked, 'I don't suppose anyone has arranged any free time for Emily?' She glanced out of the window to the frost-covered garden and the trees and shrubs under a wintry sky. 'It will soon be Christmas; she might like to look at the shops.'

'She could ask.'

'Of course, but somehow I don't think she would do that.'

Mr van Tecqx made his way upstairs and tapped on Emily's door. She was sitting on the window seat, one leg curled under her, and the face she turned to him was unknowingly wistful.

He came and sat down beside her. 'Emily, I had no intention of being discourteous just now, although it must seem so to you. I thought you might like half an hour to yourself. Tell me, have you been out at all?'

'Into the town, no, but I've been in the garden several times a day.'

He made an impatient gesture. 'I'm sorry, I should have arranged your free time before I went away—a day off a week and at least two hours to yourself each day. Lucillia is difficult and demanding. Shall we wipe the slate clean? Have a free day tomorrow and do what you like. Come and go as you please. I'll tell Bas, then you can have your meals when you want them. From now on you must be free after lunch for two hours at least. Lucillia is coming along very nicely even in the short time in which you have been here, it's time she began to stand on her own two feet, in more senses than one.'

'Thank you, but who will get Lucillia out of bed in the morning? I'll go when I've done that...'

'My mother is staying for a day or two, she and Anneke can manage tomorrow; I can do any lifting. Let us have no arguing.'

He went unhurriedly to the door. 'You will be going out this afternoon, of course. Lucillia will be having lunch downstairs—you too. If you could settle her for her nap afterwards? We should leave the house by two o'clock.'

Lucillia was disposed to be peevish when the time came for her to go to her room and rest, but her brother bore her inexorably upstairs with Emily behind, sat her down on her bed, warned her that Sint Nicolaas would leave no presents for her unless she did exactly as Emily told her, and went away, leaving Emily to make her charge comfortable—no easy task, for Lucillia was determined to grumble at everything and everyone. It was almost two o'clock by the time Emily escaped to her own room, crammed her woolly hat on to her hastily brushed hair, got into her coat and joined the party in the hall, where she greeted everyone a little shyly before being hurried out of the house by the twins.

They hadn't far to go. A few minutes' walk brought them to where was the Markt with the Nieuwe Kerk at one end of it and the Stadhuis at the other. The vast square was lined with people, but Mr van Tecqx had a long friendship with the *burgermeester* so that his party were able to take up a splendid position close to the Stadhuis. Emily, her face glowing with excitement and cold, had been urged to stand with the children so that she might have a good view, and she cheered and clapped with the best of them when the town band marched into the square, followed by the town's dignitaries and finally by the Saint himself, riding on a splendid white horse, his bishop's mitre glistening in the winter sunshine, his scarlet robes spread around him. Zwarte Piet walked beside him, armed with his birch broom and his sack, ready to pop any naughty child into its depths. There was a good deal of laughter and shouting and singing too, and Mr van Tecqx, leaning his bulk against a pillar of the Stadhuis, watched Emily and smiled at her animated little face. And his three sisters, standing close by, watched him and exchanged raised eyebrows and amused smiles. They were a close-knit family and for years they had presented suitable young women to him in the hope of his marrying again, with absolutely no success. He had many friends, several women among them, but even the most attractive of them had failed to touch his heart. He had made no secret of his bargain with Emily, but as far as they could see he treated her in much the same manner as he would adopt towards a Ward Sister in any of the hospitals he visited.

They trooped back to tea presently, and Emily hurried to Lucillia's room to make sure that she was ready to go downstairs. Mevrouw van Tecqx was sitting with her daughter, and they spent a few minutes plying Emily with questions about the procession before the older lady went away and Emily got Lucillia ready to go to the tea-party. Mr van Tecqx came presently and carried her downstairs, and at the same time he bade Emily accompany them.

'Sint Nicolaas will leave a sack of presents for the children as soon as tea is finished—the twins have outgrown him, of course, but the other children do still believe in him.'

Tea was a noisy affair, and Emily, sitting quietly and saying little, thought what a pity it was that Mr van Tecqx wasn't married with a family of his own; his house was so exactly right for children.

Tea over, there was a thunderous knock on the front door and Bas went to answer it, to return with a bulging and heavy sack which he solemnly assured the company had been left by the Saint. The children, round-eyed, crowded round while their uncle untied the sack and proceeded to hand out the brightly wrapped packages. Everyone had something; the room was littered with coloured paper and boxes as the younger ones examined their presents, while the family grown-ups exclaimed with suitable surprise at Sint Nicolaas's uncanny powers of giving just what was wanted. The ladies opened their presents next; Emily, clasping a thin, square box wrapped in tissue paper and tied with bright ribbons, watched while each in turn disclosed their gifts: gold chains, earrings, a sparkling diamond brooch, and for Lucillia the chain she had been promised to match her earrings. Only

when they had all done did Mevrouw van Tecqx ask
Emily kindly if she wasn't going to open her own gift.

Handkerchiefs, a dozen of the finest lawn, lace-
trimmed and delicately embroidered. Mr van Tecqx,
watching her from under his lids, saw the delight on her
face and her wide smile. The handkerchiefs, when he
had told Jessica to buy something suitable, had seemed
just right when she had shown them to him, but now he
frowned. The contrast between his sisters' costly gifts
and Emily's struck him as being almost cruel.

Emily had no such qualms. She was touched and
grateful that she had been included in the present-giving,
especially as she had contributed nothing herself. The
handkerchiefs were the finest she had ever possessed,
and since everyone else had solemnly thanked Sint
Nicolaas for their presents, she did the same.

Bas came in with champagne then with Anneke and
the housemaids behind him, and everyone drank the
Saint's health, and presently the children were led away
to have their hands washed and to be tidied for dinner.
Dinner was to be early so that they could stay up and
have it with the grown-ups, and it was when they had
gone that Lucillia declared pettishly that she was too
tired to stay downstairs any longer. 'I'm going to bed,'
she declared. 'I'll have dinner on a tray. Emily must have
it with me.'

Mr van Tecqx said, at his most reasonable, 'I should
think Emily might dine with us—it is a special occasion.'

Lucillia burst into angry tears. 'What about me? Be
by myself? I'm just left alone all day. . .'

'You are tired,' said her brother kindly, and proffered
a handkerchief to mop her face. 'When you are in bed
and feeling rested you will cheer up.'

'No, I won't!' Lucillia's voice had become shrill; she was working herself into a tantrum. Emily, standing silently by, spoke.

'I'm quite tired too,' she declared cheerfully. 'I'll have dinner with you and you can explain the feast of Sint Nicolaas to me—I've got a bit confused.'

Mr van Tecqx had, for some reason he hadn't examined too closely, been anticipating with some pleasure Emily's presence at his table that evening. He frowned, but when Lucillia's lip quivered ominously he said calmly, 'Very well, my dear, but let me make it quite clear: Emily is to have a day to herself tomorrow and nothing—I repeat, nothing—is to alter that.'

Lucillia peeped at him over the handkerchief. When Sebastian spoke in that quiet voice she had learnt that he meant what he said. She whispered, 'All right, Sebastian, I promise I'll be good.'

Emily, helping her patient to bed, arranging everything just so and then sitting down to eat her dinner at a small table Bas had arranged for her near the bed, could hear the cheerful voices and laughter, sounding muted from downstairs, and longed to be there too, but there was no point in wanting something she couldn't have, and she had the whole day to herself on the morrow. She carried on a cheerful conversation with Lucillia, and once dinner was finished, settled her against her pillows, fetched *Vanity Fair* and started to read. Half an hour later Lucillia was asleep, and Emily closed the book and sat there doing nothing. It was too early to go to bed and she didn't like to go downstairs. The room was warm and she longed suddenly for a breath of air, and she wondered if anything would be said if she were to put on her coat and spend a few minutes in the garden.

They would think she was mad, walking around in the dark on a cold winter's night.

When the door opened silently she turned quickly, her finger to her lips. It was Mr van Tecqx. For a man of his size and weight he moved lightly. He bent over his sister and crossed to Emily's chair, to bend down and speak softly into her ear.

'You have had a busy day—half an hour's brisk walk will do us both good. Everyone is going home very shortly, so come down and say goodnight first.'

'Suppose Lucillia wakes up?'

'Mama will be here.' He caught her by the hand and pulled her gently from her chair, and still holding her hand, went downstairs. There was a good deal of cheerful bustle going on in the hall, with sleepy children being buttoned into coats and wrapped in scarves. The baby in his Moses basket slept peacefully while hands were shaken and kisses exchanged, and Emily was urged to visit Sebastian's sisters. 'Just let us know, and someone will come and fetch you,' they told her in turn, and, 'If you can't manage it before Christmas, we shall all see you then.'

With the last car gone, the house seemed very quiet. Mevrouw van Tecqx went back to the drawing-room and sank into an easy chair. 'How pleasant to have all the family all at the same time, but I must confess I'm tired.'

'Then close your eyes for half an hour,' suggested her son. 'Emily and I are going for a short walk; we both feel the need of some fresh air. Lucillia is asleep, but I'll warn Anneke as we go.'

'What a good idea, Sebastian—the streets will be quiet too; everyone will be at home this evening.'

He ushered Emily into the hall, the dogs at his heels. 'We'll get you something warm to put on—no need to go upstairs again. I must speak to Anneke.'

He swept her along, through the door to the kitchen where Anneke produced a thick hooded cloak which she draped round Emily's shoulders. It was a good deal too big, hanging down to her ankles, its folds completely concealing her. Mr van Tecqx didn't laugh, but she was sure he was secretly amused at the sight of her. He bent down and fastened the hood under her chin, got his coat and ushered her out of the front door.

The cold air took her breath, but only for a moment. The street was quiet, the steeple roofs of the houses glistening with frost under a pale moon, the canal glistening lelly under it. Mr van Tecqx took her arm beneath the cloak and marched her briskly to the end of the silent street and over an arched bridge into another narrow street with another bridge at its end. Emily recognised the Stadhuis as they skirted one end of the Markt, but they didn't stop.

'Too dark to see much,' observed her companion. 'We will go as far as the Oude Kerk and Sint Agathaplein.'

Emily, trotting to keep up with his long strides, had little breath to reply. She contented herself with seeing all that she could. In the moonlight the houses they passed appeared to be straight out of the Middle Ages. She drew sufficient breath to say so and was told good-humouredly that that was exactly when they had been built. She saved her breath then until they reached the Oude Kerk and just beyond the cloister gardens. In summer, she was told, they were a splendid sight, and even in winter they were a haven of peace and quiet, in spite of the fact that busy Phoenisstraat was on the other side of the garden. Mr van Tecqx stopped in the shadow of the Oude Kerk's mighty tower. 'I should have enjoyed taking you round Delft, but unfortunately I shall be in Amsterdam tomorrow. I will tell Bas to give you a map so that you can find your way easily. Have you sufficient money?'

Emily peered up at him from the depths of the hood. 'Yes, thank you—I got some money changed before I left England.'

'If you want to lunch out, any of the coffee shops are good.' He took her arm again. 'We will go back along Oude Delft.'

There were more little bridges to cross until they reached the narrow cobbled way beside the canal, and presently crossed it once more to reach a bewildering network of lanes and streets, although, Mr van Tecqx pointed out, it was pretty difficult to lose oneself, for there was always the Nieuwe Kerk towering above the rooftops.

Outside his front door once more Emily paused to say politely, 'Thank you, Mr van Tecqx, I enjoyed that very much.'

He paused, the door key in his hand. 'So did I.' He stared down at her nice little face, framed in the thick hood. 'You look quite charming in that thing.' He bent and kissed her, then straightened up, smiling.

She went past him as he opened the door. It was the moonlight, she supposed, and perhaps he had had too much champagne. She took the cloak off, and he took it from her and cast it on a chair. She thought soberly that she had discarded the gentle delight of their walk with that garment; she was Lucillia's nurse once more, fulfilling her side of the bargain.

Bas appeared silently, bearing a tray of coffee which he carried into the drawing-room, and Emily murmured goodnight and made for the staircase.

'Not so fast!' Mr van Tecqx sounded amused. 'You must have a warm drink after that freezing air,' and he propelled her into the room where Mevrouw was still sitting.

She put down the book she was reading. 'Well, did you enjoy your walk? Is Delft not beautiful in the moonlight, Emily?'

Emily agreed, and Mr van Tecqx said nothing at all, but sat in his chair drinking his coffee and listening to his mother's easy chatter. Emily had very little to say for herself either, and presently, after what she hoped was a suitable interval, she said goodnight and went to her bed.

Lucillia was still sleeping soundly. Emily wondered if she would be difficult in the morning; she would have to say good morning to her before she left the house. She would spend the day exploring. By day Delft would be just as beautiful and much easier to see. Mr van Tecqx would be an excellent guide, she reflected sleepily, but if ever—and it wasn't likely—she found herself out with him again she would have to take care to keep her distance. His kisses, lightly given, were a little disconcerting.

CHAPTER SIX

RATHER to Emily's surprise, Mevrouw van Tecqx was already at breakfast when she went downstairs. 'I don't see a great deal of Sebastian,' she explained, 'so I came down early so that we might have a little talk before he left. I am so glad that he will be at home for a few weeks; he goes back to London in January, I believe.' She poured coffee for Emily and handed her the cup and saucer. 'You have no plans, my dear? Lucillia is making good progress, is she not, but you are not counting on leaving us before she is in better heart?'

Emily laid a slice of cheese on her bread. 'No, *mevrouw*, I told Mr van Tecqx I would stay as long as I was needed. That was the bargain we made. I can never repay him for operating on Father...'

'Oh, I think that is mistaken on your part, child. You are more than repaying him. Where do you plan to go first today?'

'Well, there's so much to see—I thought the Nieuwe Kerk first, then the Oude Kerk, and then I'll walk about and get my bearings. Mr van Tecqx told me I can get lunch in any of the coffee shops, and then I'll look at the shops for a while...'

'It gets dark early, you must come back when you wish. Bas will get you tea if you would like that, and of course you will dine with us. Sebastian will be back soon after six o'clock. If you want to stay out for tea, there is a charming little café at one side of the Markt; go

108

through the shop into the little room beyond; it will be quiet, and the cakes are delicious.'

Emily poked her head round Lucillia's door before she left the house and found her sitting up in bed eating her breakfast. 'I'm just off,' she said. 'I'll look in the shop windows and study the fashions and tell you all about them when I get back.'

She whisked herself away quickly before Lucillia could say more than goodbye.

Armed with the street map Bas had pressed upon her, she set out. The Markt was close by and to her delight it was market day. There were stalls everywhere, selling everything. It was still early, but they were already busy, and Emily roamed around, admiring the flowers and fruit and the rows of undergarments, vivid blankets and material by the yard blowing in the strong wind. The Nieuwe Kerk—and not so new, since it had been built in the fourteenth century—was vast and, so early in the day, almost empty of people. Emily wandered up and down and spent quite a time contemplating the mausoleum of the murdered William of Orange and the monuments to the House of Orange, a great many of them lying in the vaults below the choir. She left at last and found her way to Oude Delft and so to the Oude Kerk, built a century earlier, painstakingly restored; there were any number of magnificent tombs here too, and the great bell in the Oude Kerk Tower, which, according to the English guide book she found in the church, was only tolled for great joy or deep sorrow.

It was only a step to Sint Agathaklooster and the gardens. She stood looking around her, thinking of the previous evening with Mr van Tecqx. It was too cold to stand still for long, so she walked back the way she had

come and found a coffee shop and then, much re-
freshed, walked to the Huis Lambert van Meerten, a
museum housing Delftware and antique furniture. It was
pleasant not to have to hurry or look at the clock. It
was well past noon when she went back to the coffee
shop she had discovered earlier and had more coffee and
a *kass broodje* before setting off once more, this time
to look at the shops. She spent a long time strolling round
Reynders, on the edge of the Markt, which sold genuine
Delftware. When she had some money, she decided, she
would buy a cup and a saucer, or perhaps a plate, and
take them back for her father, and a little vase for Mrs
Philips.

There were some stylish dress shops too, although
Lucillia had told her she always went to den Haag for
her clothes. Emily, pressing her unpretentious nose
against the plate glass, would have been happy enough
to enter any of them and fit herself out. It was growing
dark by now, although it wasn't yet four o'clock. Time
for tea, she decided, and found her way to the café
Mevrouw van Tecqx had mentioned. Some of the tables
were occupied, but she found one to herself and asked
for tea and cakes. The cakes were very large, smothered
in cream and simply delicious; Emily lingered over the
small meal and then walked back to Mr van Tecqx's
house, pausing frequently to look in the shop windows.
Presently she had left the Markt and the lighted streets
behind her and entered the quiet world of cobbled ways
beside small canals and old, beautifully restored houses.
She paused on the steps of the house before she rang the
bell and looked around her. The street was quiet, light
from the windows reflected in the quiet water of the
canal. It was cold; her breath streamed out in a halo

around her and she could smell the frost in the air. It would be another lovely moonlit night. She wondered about Mr van Tecqx, driving back from Amsterdam after a day's work. Doing what, she wondered—operating perhaps, or examining or teaching? She sighed and wished she knew more about him.

Bas opened the door in answer to her ring. He beamed at her in his kindly fashion and asked, 'Tea, miss?'

Emily shook her head. 'No, thank you, Bas, I've had it.'

A remark which he seemed to understand, but she was glad to see Anneke come into the hall.

'A good day, miss? You have eaten? Dinner is at half past seven and Mevrouw is with Juffrouw Lucillia. She is good all day.' She nodded and smiled.

'I had a lovely day, thank you, Anneke. I'll go and see Lucillia when I've removed my coat.'

Emily supposed she was entitled to have the evening to herself if she had wanted it, but she had nothing to do; wandering the streets and drinking coffee at cafés was hardly her scene, and to sit in her room and read seemed a tame ending to her day. She tidied herself and went along to Lucillia's room.

She was still in her chair, leafing through a magazine, and her mother was sitting with her, knitting. They looked up as Emily went in and Lucillia gave a delighted shout. 'Emily, have you come to put me to bed? I am so tired of this chair, but I must sit until Anneke has finished in the kitchen.'

Mevrouw van Tecqx put down her knitting. 'I'm not quite strong enough to help Lucillia and I am afraid I am often clumsy.'

Emily thought she looked tired; probably Lucillia had been tiresome. 'Well, I came to see if I could take over. I can manage without Anneke and I expect she has enough to do in the kitchen.'

Mevrouw van Tecqx cast her a grateful look. 'That would be kind of you, Emily, but you are still free, you know.'

'Yes—well, I'll just see to Lucillia, it won't take long and I haven't anything else to do.'

'You enjoyed your day?'

'Oh, yes, indeed I did. Delft is an enchanting town, and it's small enough to find one's way easily.'

Mevrouw van Tecqx went away and Emily began on the business of getting Lucillia into her bed. It took a good deal longer than usual, for she was reluctant to use her crutches, declaring the physiotherapist had hurt her abominably that morning. 'She made me walk too much. I don't know why she bothers; I shall never walk properly again.'

'Well, now that's a pity, because I had an idea while I was out. I can't see why one day soon we shouldn't go for a walk round the shops. I can manage the chair, only of course you may need to take a step or two if we stop for coffee or to buy something.'

Emily had Lucillia's full attention now. 'Emily, you mean that? But I don't suppose Sebastian would allow it.'

'Well, I don't mean straight away—in a week or two perhaps: we need not go far at first, but you'll need to work hard at your exercises and forget all your worries about not walking properly again. Of course you will; it's a question of time and patience, both boring, I know, but if only you can make up your mind that you'll be as good as new...'

She arranged Lucillia in bed and wheeled the bed-table close ready for the tray, and when Anneke came bustling in with it she waited only long enough to make sure that her patient had all she wanted before going to make herself presentable before going downstairs. It was also almost half past seven, and for all she knew Mr van Tecqx was already home; the house was big enough to smother any sound from below, and she would hate to keep him waiting. On the other hand, she didn't want to make an uneasy third in the drawing-room.

She had reached the bottom of the staircase when the front door opened and he came in, bringing a rush of cold air with him. He put his bag down and threw his coat on to a chair.

'Hello, I'm almost late, aren't I? Be a good girl and pour me a drink while I wash and say good day to Lucillia.' He went past her, but half-way up the stairs stopped and turned round. 'Did you have a good day?'

'Yes, thank you. What do you want to drink, Mr van Tecqx?'

'Whisky—two fingers and a little water.'

Emily went into the drawing-room and found his mother sitting by the blazing fire, her knitting in her lap. She looked up as Emily went in and said, 'Sebastian is back? Bas got me a drink, my dear, will you help yourself from the tray?'

'Thank you, *mevrouw*. Mr van Tecqx asked me to pour him a whisky.'

She did it carefully and put the glass on the tray on the lamp table by his chair just as he came into the room. He shut the door behind him and stood watching her for a moment. In her plain woollen dress she was really not worth a second glance, and yet she had an aura of content and quiet which was most soothing after a long day in the operating theatre.

'That looks good,' he observed. 'Have you a drink, Emily? What can I get you?'

She turned to look at him, smiling a little; her face was slightly flushed and her lovely eyes sparkled. Just for a moment in the soft light of the lovely room, she looked beautiful. 'Sherry, please.' Her voice was a delight too... Sebastian poured the sherry, smiling cynically; he must be tired to allow such an absurd thought to enter his head. He gave her the sherry and went to sit down and engage his mother in small talk until Bas came to tell them that dinner was served.

Emily excused herself soon after they had finished and had their coffee; Lucillia would expect her to tuck her up for the night even though she was technically free until the morning, and Mr van Tecqx made no demur when she did so. He wished her a polite goodnight, opened the door for her and shut it behind her with something of a snap, so that his mother gave him a thoughtful look as he sat himself down again. She was far too wise to say anything, merely remarked on the pleasure of the Sint Nicolaas evening. 'So quickly over,' she observed, 'but how the children love it! I think Emily enjoyed herself very much—she is good with children, isn't she?'

He settled in his chair. 'They're nice children,' he said blandly. 'I'll have to leave early in the morning, Mama— you will forgive me if I am not here when you go home? The car will come for you?'

'Yes, thank you, dear. Have you a busy day again?'

'In Amsterdam, yes. I'm taking Beatrix van Telle out to dinner in the evening.'

'Such a charming woman,' observed his mother sweetly. 'Now tell me, what plans have you made for Christmas?'

By the end of the following day Emily wondered wearily if this was to be the pattern every time she had a day off. Lucillia had been as unco-operative as she knew how. The physiotherapist had fulfilled her task with a wooden expression and heaved an audible sigh when her session was over. At least she could go away, thought Emily, faced with a virago who alternately wept and raged at her, refused to eat and made life a misery for anyone who came near her. Luckily her mother had gone home soon after breakfast and Mr van Tecqx was away long before that. Emily bore the brunt of her patient's ill humour, preserving a calm face and unending patience, but by the evening she was worn out, and when Mr van Tecqx arrived back home and meeting her in the hall, bearing a tray laden with her patient's supper, enquired how his sister did, all she could say with a wooden face was that Lucillia hadn't had a good day.

He took the tray from her and put it down on a console table, and gave her a thoughtful look. She was pale and tired, her hair had had no attention for some time and her nose shone. 'You haven't had a good day either,' he said, and when she went to pick up the tray, 'No, leave that, I shall take it up. Go into the drawing-room and wait for me there, Emily.'

Emily did as she had been told. She was really too tired to argue, anyway, and to sit down in the quiet room was bliss. She was actually on the point of dropping off when he returned, poured her a drink and put it into her hand. 'I gather from Bas that Lucillia has been playing up?'

Emily nodded and gulped at her sherry. 'Perhaps I'm not...' she began, and then, 'It may have been a mistake, choosing me. I mean, I think I'm not good enough. I'm so sorry—I've done my best and I truly like Lucillia—I thought we were making headway too.'

Mr van Tecqx sat himself in his chair, a glass of whisky in his hand. 'So what do you propose that I should do?' he wanted to know. He seemed unconcerned.

'Well, perhaps you ought to find someone with more experience than I have.'

'You wish to throw in the sponge?'

She sat up very straight. 'Of course not! It's a challenge, isn't it?! But it isn't me that matters...' Mr van Tecqx winced at the grammar, but she didn't notice. 'It's getting Lucillia well again—she needs something to make her make the effort and forget that she's been ill. She needs to have her mind taken off that, and I'm not enough.'

Mr van Tecqx stared down at the glass in his hand. 'Let us get something straight. You have done a great deal for Lucillia. I knew that you were the right person for her, and you are. You feel a failure because you have borne the brunt of her impatience and frustration, but you have by no means failed, Emily. Will you hang on, however tiring she is? I will think of something—you are quite right, she needs something or someone to give her that final impetus...'

Emily put down her glass; the sherry had gone to her head and she was in no fit state to disagree with anything Mr van Tecqx might suggest.

'Very well, Mr van Tecqx, and thank you. I'll go back to Lucillia...'

'No, you won't. I have told her that you are dining with me. She is eating her dinner and had the grace to agree with me that you needed food as much as anyone.'

He got up and tugged at the old-fashioned bell rope by the side of the fireplace, and when Bas arrived he asked if dinner could be put forward half an hour. He then poured a second glass of sherry for Emily, observed that he would be back very shortly and left the room.

She sipped her drink, aware that it was a silly thing to do since she had had very little to eat all day. By the time he came back she was half asleep, but with an effort she made conversation until Bas came to say that dinner had been served.

They were half-way through their soup when Bas went to answer the telephone and came back to say that Juffrouw van Telle was wanting to know if she was to be picked up as arranged. As he spoke in Dutch Emily didn't understand him, but she was aware of Mr van Tecqx's quick frown as he excused himself and left the table. He came back a few minutes later and embarked at once on a gentle stream of talk which gave nothing away as to his true feelings, which, Emily privately considered, were vexatious to say the least.

They had their coffee at the table, and presently she went back upstairs to find a chastened Lucillia. She was barely inside the room when her troublesome patient cried, 'Emily, you won't go away, will you? Sebastian says you will if I can't stop behaving like a spoilt baby. He's not often angry, you know, but just for a little while he was. He said you were a treasure and he'd never find your equal, even if he searched the world over.'

Emily felt a pleasant glow; it was more than pleasant, it was exciting too, although she didn't know why; it was doused almost at once as Lucillia went on, 'He says you're the best nurse he has had to deal with for years.'

'How very kind,' said Emily in a flat voice. What on earth had possessed her, even momentarily, to suppose he had meant anything else?

She saw very little of Mr van Tecqx during the next few days, but she did meet Juffrouw van Telle, who came to visit Lucillia, bringing with her an armful of books and a bunch of hothouse flowers which she thrust at Emily with an abrupt request that they should be put in water instantly.

As she did so, Emily was conscious of the fact that she was being studied closely. 'You are Lucillia's nurse?' enquired Juffrouw van Telle, stating the obvious. 'You don't look very strong.'

Her English was good and Emily thought for the hundredth time since she had come to Holland what a disadvantage it was when everyone seemed to speak her own language as well as she did herself, while she had difficulty in making sense of even the simplest sentence in Dutch.

What to answer? She could, of course, flex her muscles or give a demonstration of how she got Lucillia in and out of bed, not so much by the use of strength as by knowing how to do it properly. She contented herself with a smile which was wiped off her face as she left the room and heard Juffrouw van Telle's rather shrill voice exclaim in English, 'But, my dear Lucillia, what a very plain girl!'

Emily slowed her footsteps and unashamedly eavesdropped. The visitor gave a tinkling laugh. 'You know,

I was a little uneasy when Sebastian told me he wouldn't be able to dine the other evening because he felt he should remain at home. When I asked him why he said it was because your nurse was in need of support—I pictured some lovely English rose flirting with him, but I see I wasted my concern.'

Emily trod silently down to the kitchen, where she begged a vase from Anneke, rammed the flowers in in a ruthless fashion and accepted a cup of coffee from the housekeeper.

It was her own fault for listening, of course, but she felt a little better when Anneke said, 'It is Juffrouw van Telle who visits? When our Lucillia was so ill, she came not she is afraid, you understand, that she is ill also.' She shook her head. 'Not good.'

Emily longed to agree, but if Mr van Tecqx was in love with the woman it seemed disloyal. She murmured non-committally, thanked Anneke for her coffee and went back upstairs.

It struck her as she entered the room that Lucillia didn't like her visitor. Her face was a polite blank, the same face which her brother assumed at times. She was sitting in her chair by the window and cast a speaking look at Emily, who rose to the occasion with the first thing she could think of.

'It's time for your physio, Lucillia,' she said, all of a sudden very professional, and added cunningly, 'Would you care to stay and watch, Juffrouw van Telle?'

'No, no. I find it so painful to see Lucillia so crippled, and I dare say it exhausts her.' She bent to brush Lucillia's cheek with a meaningless kiss, nodded carelessly at Emily and went away in a little rush.

'Dear, kind Emily,' said Lucillia. 'I do not like that woman and she doesn't like me. Do you know that when I was first ill she wouldn't come and see me? And when Sebastian brought me here she was afraid that the whole house would be con—con-...'

'Contaminated,' finished Emily.

'And I am not a cripple!'

'Well, of course you're not, but you know people who are scared of illness never know anything about it. It would be very nice if next time she comes you're downstairs leaning negligently against something!'

That made Lucillia laugh. 'She used to come here quite a lot, that was before I was ill and I lived with Mama, but when I came to see Sebastian she was always ringing up or wanting something, but she doesn't come often nowadays. She doesn't like you.'

Emily received this news with equanimity. 'Who cares about that? Now how about those exercises?'

It was the following day that Mr van Tecqx arrived home in the middle of the day—something he seldom did. He had someone with him. Emily had just got Lucillia downstairs and into the drawing-room; it had taken a very long time, but now, flushed with their triumph, Lucillia was sitting by the fire while Emily nipped back to fetch a light rug.

Emily had chosen the afternoon in which to try out her plan; there would be no one about until Bas brought in the tea and no one would come unless she rang. Lucillia struggled to the top of the stairs and then submitted to being sat down on the top step. With Emily beside her ready with a supporting arm, she had bumped her way down to the bottom. The two of them giggled a good deal while they made their slow progress; it was an undignified way in which to gain the hall, but at least Lucillia did it finally, and after a rest, she crossed the hall on her crutches to the safety of the drawing-room chair.

Emily heard the murmur of voices as she raced back down the staircase; probably Bas making up the fire. She opened the door with a flourish—and stopped short at the sight of Mr van Tecqx, leaning against a sofa table listening intently to Lucillia. Standing beside him was a young man, a head shorter than he, with a pleasant and rather rugged face and dark hair. He was staring at Lucillia and she was staring back, and Mr van Tecqx was watching them both, his bland mask of a face shielding his thoughts. He looked up as Emily came to an abrupt halt.

'Ah, Emily.' There was nothing in his quiet voice to tell her if he were annoyed or pleased to see his sister downstairs. 'I see that you have wrought a miracle. A delightful surprise. May I present Dr ter Beule, who has just taken up a houseman's post in Leiden? A very promising pupil of mine.'

Emily shook hands and murmured, and retired discreetly out of Mr van Tecqx's line of fire; she was never very happy when he addressed her in such silky tones. 'Tea?' he enquired gently, and she tugged the bell rope.

The tea tray was carried in within minutes and Emily, asked to pour out, did so. Dr ter Beule had drawn up a chair close to Lucillia and they were deep in conversation. Mr van Tecqx had taken his usual chair and spoke only when spoken to, which Emily, left behind the teapot, found worrying, and she tried to make up her mind whether to engage him in small talk or keep quiet.

As she couldn't think of any small talk anyway, she stayed silent, handing teacups and passing plates of cake and biscuits, all the time aware that Mr van Tecqx was watching her.

She offered second cups and presently said, 'You will excuse me? There are several...'

She got no further. 'I'm sure Dirk can entertain Lucillia for ten minutes or so, Emily. Perhaps you would be good enough to come to my study?'

The other two hardly noticed as they left the room. He held the door open for her as they reached his study and offered her a chair before sitting down behind his desk.

'Do tell me,' he begged her coolly, 'just how did you get Lucillia downstairs? Bas was obviously surprised to see her when he brought the tea. Who helped you?'

'Well, no one, actually. She managed on her crutches to the staircase and then I helped her sit down to rest on the top stair. After which I sat beside her and put an arm round her and we worked—our way down to the hall.'

'On your bottoms?'

Emily flushed faintly. 'Yes.'

'And then?'

'Lucillia walked on her crutches to her chair in the drawing-room.'

'And what inspired her—and you—to do that?'

It was rather like being cross-examined by someone who knew he was going to get the better of her anyway. She said defiantly, 'Juffrouw van Telle came to see Lucillia yesterday. I'm quite sure she didn't mean to be unkind——' she crossed her fingers behind her back as she said it, for it was a fib, 'but she called Lucillia a cripple and Lucillia was most upset, so I thought it might be a good idea.' She studied the bland face on the other side of the desk. 'And it was,' she said firmly. 'And now the nice young man has turned up and they like each other, and that's just what she needs.'

He said equably, 'Yes, I thought so too. I was a student with his elder brother, so it will be quite an easy matter for him to have the run of the house. My mother knew him as a small boy, my sisters too—a family friend. But he and Lucillia have never met.'

'Oh,' her fine eyes sparkled, 'wouldn't it be great if they were to—to like each other?'

'Fall in love?' he amended coolly. 'Yes, most suitable.' He shifted in his chair, his eyes on her face. 'You took a risk this afternoon, Emily. Repeat the exercise by all means, but take care to have someone with you.' He looked at her curiously. 'Were you not frightened?'

'Oh, my goodness, yes, but you see I had to do something to make her see that she's as normal as you or I.'

He agreed gravely, 'Of course. You have had your free time this afternoon?'

'Well, not really—you see, it took a long time, getting Lucillia down, and I couldn't leave her sitting there, could I?'

'No. So we will leave the two young people to get to know each other and you and I will take a brisk walk. You have not yet seen the grave of Louis the Seventeenth at the far end of the Oude Delft? Good. Fetch your coat and put something on your head. It is a cold day.'

Emily got into her coat, crammed her woolly hat on her neat head, found her gloves and went downstairs. Mr van Tecqx was in the hall, coated and gloved and bareheaded. He gave her a cursory glance, opened his house door and ushered her outside.

'I shall take you first to see the grave and then we will walk back along the Oude Delft; there are some rather interesting antique shops there.'

She agreed meekly, feeling it would have made little difference to his plans if she had suggested going somewhere else.

It was bitingly cold with a bitter wind and Mr van Tecqx marched along at a great rate, a hand tucked under her elbow so that she had perforce to keep up with him. She was quite out of breath by the time they reached the wrought iron railing which surrounded the grave. The inscription was in French and she read it out loud, and added, 'How sad. Do you suppose he really was Louis the Sixteenth's son?'

'We shall never know. There was a will, left by the Duchess of Angoulême, which should have thrown some light on the matter, but it has been lost.'

She touched the fleurs-de-lys which adorned the railings. 'So it may be a king buried here?'

'We like to think so.' He turned her smartly round and headed back along the Oude Delft. As they walked a few flakes of snow drifted lazily down, barely disturbing the grey water of the canal.

'You should have worn a hat,' said Emily.

He had tucked a hand under her elbow again. 'I have never met a girl like you before,' he observed. It was impossible to tell from his voice whether he had meant that in a complimentary sense or not; she thought it prudent to say nothing.

The antique shops were delightful. Emily peered into their small, crowded windows, admiring the bric-à-brac, the old silver and the beautiful bags, all beaded, that bygone housewives had worn attached to their belts. There were gold earrings and heavy brooches and silver clasps and head ornaments. She lingered from one shop to the next, until she happened to glance up and saw that Mr van Tecqx's bare head was lightly covered with snow.

'I'm so sorry—it's awfully kind of you to stand about. I quite forgot...'

He only smiled and then walked her briskly on back to the house, where they parted in the hall. 'Perhaps you will be good enough to come down and collect Lucillia's odds and ends—I'll carry her up to her room.'

He sounded aloof and she said quietly, 'Yes, Mr van Tecqx, I'll be down in five minutes.'

But when she went to the drawing-room she found that Lucillia had other ideas. To go back to bed just as she was getting to know Dirk didn't please her at all.

'We have to go back to Leiden this evening,' her brother pointed out patiently. 'We are both working men, *liefje*. Dirk can keep you company whenever he likes—that is if he gets enough free time.'

She looked at the younger man. 'Will you come, Dirk?'

'Of course.' He lapsed into Dutch and Emily saw Lucillia go a pretty pink and Mr van Tecqx smile slowly.

'I'll be down at once, Dirk.' He plucked his sister off her chair and carried her up to her room, with Emily trailing behind with the crutches and rug. He wasted no time. He kissed Lucillia on her cheek, murmured something to her so that she laughed, nodded to Emily and went away. A few moments later Emily heard the door close.

Lucillia couldn't have had a better incentive to get well. She talked about Dirk as Emily got her into bed; she had learned a considerable amount about him in the few hours he had been in the house and she repeated it all to Emily. 'Do you believe in love at first sight?' she wanted to know.

Emily thought. 'Well, yes, I think I do, although I'm sure you can fall in love slowly and not know until it hits you suddenly. I mean, you can feel instantly at home with some people, as though you've known them all your life.' She paused; she had felt like that the very first time she and Mr van Tecqx had met. There were exceptions to every rule, she thought regretfully.

'You look sad,' said Lucillia. 'Have you ever been in love, Emily?'

Emily opened her mouth, intending to say no, then closed it again, because that would not be true; she had been in love, she was in love at that very moment, only she had only just realised it. Essentially a truthful girl, she said, 'Yes.' It was a bit silly to admit it, because Mr van Tecqx had no more intention of falling in love with her than he had of giving up a successful surgeon's career and taking up knitting.

'Tell me about him,' said Lucillia instantly.

'There's nothing to tell,' observed Emily tranquilly. 'He doesn't know, and he certainly doesn't love me.'

'Where did you meet him?' demanded her companion.

'In England! If you don't mind, I don't want to talk about it.' Emily added brightly, 'I'd much rather talk about Dirk. How long has he been qualified?'

A red herring which was instantly swallowed. Dirk was discussed at great length and from every aspect until Bas came with Lucillia's supper tray and Emily went downstairs to her lonely dinner.

Lucillia was tired and, for once, content; she didn't want to be read to and consented to be tucked up for the night as soon as Emily went back upstairs, which left Emily with time on her hands and leisure to reflect upon her feelings for Mr van Tecqx. It would be nice if she could suppress them or at least banish them to the back of her mind, but she did neither. Telling herself she would have to be sensible about the matter, she sat down to think it over. An hour later she was still sitting there with only one clear thought in her head; she had fallen in love with Mr van Tecqx and wished above all things to be his wife.

'That's as far as you'll get, my girl,' she told herself, nodding at a van Tecqx ancestor staring at her from his portrait with cold haughtiness. 'So we'll forget the whole silly business.'

Before she began on the difficult business of forgetting, she had a good cry before she slept.

CHAPTER SEVEN

IT WAS a really good thing that Emily barely glimpsed Mr van Tecqx for the next couple of days. Indeed, it seemed as though he was deliberately avoiding her, leaving his house in the morning with a brisk, 'Good morning, Emily,' if they should happen to meet, and as for the evenings, he went straight to his study when he came home, and then went out to dinner. Emily assured herself that this was a good thing. The less notice he took of her, the easier it would be for her to quash her feelings; nip them in the bud, think about something else. Her good sense agreed with this, but she discovered that being in love didn't take good sense into account.

Her instinct was to take herself off to the shops, den Haag, even—there were trams running several times an hour—buy some dashing clothes in the first rank of fashion, have her hair permed and buy such aids to beauty as might improve her looks, but here reason took over. She had only a certain amount of money with her, and even when she received her pay cheque, she needed to save a good deal of it. Her father, even when on his two feet again, would need extra help in the house for a time at least, and she herself, even if she went straight back to Pearson's, would get no salary for a month. Besides, there was no guarantee that Mr van Tecqx would notice any difference in her appearance. True, he stared at her a good deal, but she very much doubted if he noticed her as a girl.

It was several days before she went down to breakfast and found him at the table. His 'Good morning' was genial as he got up with the unconscious good manners which she found so pleasing, begged her to help herself to coffee and toast and made trivial remarks about the weather, still holding a sheaf of papers in his hand.

She agreed that it looked like snow again, that it was very cold and that the morning was dark, even for the time of year, helped herself to toast and butter and added practically, 'Do please go on with your letters, Mr van Tecqx. I don't need to be entertained.'

'Er—was I entertaining you? I'm flattered.'

She flushed. 'You know quite well what I meant—having to be polite and talk about the weather when you have better things to do.'

He put down his letters. 'What makes you think I prefer to read my letters rather then have a conversation with you, Emily?'

When she didn't answer, the ebbing flush most annoyingly creeping back into her cheeks, he said, 'No, don't answer that. Tell me, would you like to go to den Haag and see the shops? Perhaps you wish to buy presents?'

'Yes, I should like that, but I don't mind which day I have. There's a tram, isn't there? I didn't realise that den Haag was so close. Do you give presents, just as we do?'

She paused because she was nattering on aimlessly, anxious to sound like the nurse whom he employed and not like a girl who was head over heels in love with him.

He answered her gravely, although she had the nasty feeling that he was laughing at her secretly. 'Oh, yes, we give presents and have a tree and Father Christmas.

Before the Second World War we did very little, but now we have adopted your English Christmas, although we still celebrate New Year in style.' He got to his feet. 'Well, I have a list this morning...'

At the door he paused. 'I could run you into den Haag if you would like that—the day after tomorrow?'

'That's very kind of you, but it's easy for me to go by tram.'

Emily forced herself to look at him and smile a little, but he didn't smile in return. He said shortly, 'Just as you like, Emily.'

So the following day she took the tram which travelled along the main road between Delft and den Haag and with Christmas in mind, turned her back on the Ridderzaal and the Mauritzhuis, the Geyangenpoort, the Panorama Mesdag and Madurodam, all of which Lucillia advised her that she simply had to visit, but they would have to wait for the next time, she decided, and she plunged into de Bijnenkorf, a department store which she hoped would help her to solve the problem of Christmas presents.

With the prospect of a pay packet very shortly she felt free to spend what money she had. She began cautiously with Christmas cards for her father and Mrs Philips and her friends at Pearson's, and then she began to search for something suitable to send to England. She had left it rather late and it would have to be something she could post easily. She decided on a rather dashing tie for her father and a headscarf for Mrs Philips; not very imaginative, but when she went home eventually she would be able to take a bottle of Bols *genever* for him and Dutch chocolates for her.

There was the vexed question of what to get for Lucillia and her mother, and should she choose something for Mr van Tecqx? Also, what about Bas and Anneke and the two housemaids?

Handkerchiefs, though dull, were safe. She bought cigars for Bas and hoped he smoked them. For Lucillia she bought a gossamer-fine shawl in pale blue; she already had several but had expressed a wish for something in blue. It made a great hole in Emily's purse, but the van Tecqx family appeared to have everything they wanted or wished for; not for them were the useful headscarf, the tights, the toiletries . . . she was quite sure that their scarves were of Italian silk, their tights from Dior and their toiletries from exclusive firms, where the soap alone would have cost the equivalent of a good-sized Sunday joint.

For Mevrouw van Tecqx she bought a box of marrons glacés, something she had always hankered after herself and had never had. That left her with just enough money for her fare home and a cup of coffee and a roll.

Back at the house, she wrapped her gifts carefully and wondered if she had done right not to buy anything for Mr van Tecqx. She had found a suitable card for him, but would that be enough? What could she find for someone who appeared to have everything?

She went to bed worrying about it.

It was the following afternoon, after Dirk had been to visit Lucillia and Emily had begun the laborious business of getting that young lady back into her bed, that she glanced out of the window and saw someone in the garden. It had been snowing again and although it was almost night the figure showed up darkly against the whiteness of the snow. It was a man, moving furtively towards the house, so intent on the ground-floor windows that he didn't look up to see Emily. He disappeared around the side of the house and she made rather a business of drawing the curtains, waiting to see if he returned. Which he did, going stealthily from one clump of ornamental trees to a rhododendron bush and then on to the shelter of the group of birch trees by the ornamental pool.

Lucillia was still in her chair, and Emily closed the curtains finally and said in a voice which held no hint of her disquiet, 'I've just remembered Anneke wanted to know if you fancied one of her special omelettes. You'd enjoy that, wouldn't you? I'll just pop down and tell her.'

The only person in the kitchen was one of the maids. Bas, she told Emily, had gone down to the cellars, Anneke had gone upstairs to fetch a clean apron and the other maid had a half day.

The girl spoke only Dutch; it took a few precious minutes to understand her and time, Emily considered, was of the essence. 'Tell Bas...' she began, and saw the lack of any understanding in the face of the girl. She dredged up her few words of Dutch and said, 'Pen, paper?'

When she had them, she wrote a note for Anneke in English. 'Anneke,' she said, and waved it at the girl and smiled encouragingly before letting herself out of the door beyond the various rooms beyond the kitchen.

It was dark outside, but not as dark as it had appeared from indoors. Emily stood for a minute while her eyes accustomed themselves to the night, shivering a little, for in her hurry she hadn't thought about a coat.

Only to get outside and find whoever it was and find out why he was there...

The snow was soft under her feet and she made little sound as she went round to the side of the house where she had seen the intruder. He was standing very still, peering into the drawing-room; the curtains had been drawn, but there was a small gap large enough for anyone outside to get a good view of the room. All that silver and china, thought Emily, and all he has to do is to get the french windows open.

She was filled with sudden indignation that anyone should dare. She walked quietly until she reached his hunched up back and tapped him on the shoulder.

'What do you think you're doing?' she wanted to know. 'You have no business here!'

He spun round and caught her by the arm, giving it a cruel twist. She couldn't understand a word he said, but it sounded very nasty, uttered in a rough voice, and too late she realised she had been rather silly to have challenged him on her own. It was also too late to be prudent now. She said firmly, 'Let go of my arm at once. You'd better go before I call the police.'

He took no notice, but then why should he, since he couldn't understand a word she was saying? Instead he took a firmer grip of her arm and gave it another twist. Emily gave a gasp of pain; a pity that the garden was at the back of the house, and at this side, even, where it bordered the street, there was a high brick wall, guaranteed to keep out all sound. All the same, a good scream was worth trying.

She let out a yell which gave ample proof of a very sound pair of lungs, bit the hand which instantly clamped down on her mouth, and screamed, 'Help!' at the top of her voice. The hand came down again, this time slapping her hard so that the teeth jarred in her head. But it didn't prevent her from kicking out briefly, hoping to hit something. She had caught a shin a nasty crack before the hand, balled into a fist this time, caught her a blow over her eye, and she slid on to the snow, temporarily bereft of her senses.

Mr van Tecqx, getting out of his car, heard the first yell, locked the car door and took the steps to his front door in a fine turn of speed. His hearing was excellent; the yell had come from his own garden, from the narrow strip which ran up to the brick wall which encircled it and shut it off from the street. He had his key in the door, opened it, crossed the hall and the drawing-room and flung open the french windows at the same moment as Emily's scream. It was a pity she had been knocked out, for she would have derived satisfaction from the sight of Mr van Tecqx felling her assailant with a great fist, and after a cursory glance to make sure he had knocked him out for the moment, bending over her and then plucking her out of the snow and carrying her into the drawing-room. Anneke and Bas had both arrived by then. Mr van Tecqx sent Bas to telephone the police, told Anneke to turn down Emily's bed and ordered the french windows to be closed and locked. The police would come immediately and the man was still unconscious.

Emily was small and light in his arms, and very pale. He carried her carefully upstairs and laid her on her bed, took her pulse, peered under her lids to make sure her reflexes were good and drew the coverlet over her, then sat down on the side of the bed.

She opened her eyes almost immediately and drowsily frowned at him. He wasn't very clear; her eyelid was swelling fast and before long she would have a black eye. She felt peculiar, and yet it seemed perfectly natural that Mr van Tecqx should be there. She said in a small voice, 'Hello.'

'You little fool,' said Mr van Tecqx with a kind of cold rage. 'What on earth possessed you to stick your neck out like that? You might have been killed!'

She felt sick, but she could hear the rage; it stirred her into a rage as strong as his. 'That would have been very awkward for you, wouldn't it?' she snapped at him, and burst into tears.

Mr van Tecqx took her very gently in his arms and held her securely while she grizzled into his shoulder. Presently she contrived to stop save for the odd sob. 'So sorry,' she muttered into his waistcoat.

'The best thing you could do,' he told her in a kindly, avuncular voice. 'Tears relieve an overwrought nervous system—rather like taking the lid off a saucepan of boiling water.'

Emily had managed to stop crying now, but two tears oozed down her cheeks, but not because of fright or shock any more; they were in pure sorrow, for even though Mr van Tecqx was holding her close in his arms, the only feeling she inspired in him was to liken her to a saucepan on the boil.

'Now, now,' he admonished her, 'don't start again!'

'You were so cross!' She hadn't meant her voice to sound like a wail.

He laid her carefully back on to the pillows. 'You are going to have a lovely black eye,' he told her. 'I'll get you something for it. Here is Anneke to help you, and I'll come back shortly.'

'I have no intention of going to bed,' said Emily peevishly. 'A couple of aspirin and I'll be perfectly all right.'

'You will do exactly as I say, Emily.' He turned away and spoke to Anneke, then departed. He was still angry, she thought unhappily, and submitted to Anneke's kind help. 'Is Lucillia all right?' she asked.

'I have been with her; all is well, miss, do not worry. The police are here and the man is taken.' Anneke peered closely at Emily's tearstained face. 'You have a black eye, you are also damp from the snow.' She slid Emily's nightie over her head and turned back the duvet. 'A warm bed and a glass of hot milk—I shall fetch for you.'

Mr van Tecqx's knock on the door was nicely timed. Emily was lying back with a nasty headache and a fast-closing eye. He spoke to his housekeeper, and she nodded and went away as he opened his bag and produced everything necessary for the soothing of the black eye, then shook out two pills.

'Anneke will be back with a drink, and you will take these at the same time. You should sleep soundly and you are not to get up until I have seen you in the morning.'

'Lucillia——?'

'Is perfectly all right.'

'I'm sorry I've made such a fuss and given you all so much work. You see, there wasn't time to fetch Bas or Anneke, and I was so afraid that man would get in and steal the silver.'

'Very praiseworthy of you, Emily, and very brave, but I must beg of you never to do such a thing again. I feel very much to blame, it never occurred to me to tell you that the house is protected by burglar alarms which sound off at the police station if anyone tries to enter.'

She wasn't going to cry again, even though she had to clench her teeth to stop her mouth shaking. She turned her head away, and presently he went away, giving place to Anneke bearing the hot milk and who provided a kind embrace in which Emily could weep in comfort.

Asleep within ten minutes or so, Emily was unaware of Mr van Tecqx returning soft-footed to stand by her bed, looking down at her with a kind of thoughtful surprise on his handsome features.

She felt very much better in the morning. She was even able to return his involuntary smile at the sight of her eye, now all colours of the rainbow and quite closed. In reply to his questions she affirmed that she was feeling perfectly well, that her headache had gone, which wasn't quite true, and she would like to get up.

'Very well, but first I should like to take a look at that eye and check your pulse.'

When he had done he said, 'Don't attempt to lift or heave—I know Lucillia is very light, but just for a day or so be good enough to do as I ask. Dirk ter Beule has a free day, he will be here this morning and will carry Lucillia downstairs. I imagine he will be staying for the rest of the day, so you will be able to take a rest after lunch while they entertain each other. I shall be back around six o'clock and either of us will carry her back to her room. I have asked Anneke to give you a hand with Lucillia when you get her up. Let her walk as much as she wants with her crutches once Dirk is here to walk with her.' He glanced at her, his eyebrows raised. 'You understand?'

Emily shot him a cross look from the good eye. 'Yes,' and mumbled a peevish, 'Orders, orders,' under her breath.

'Tiresome, aren't I? but I expect you to do as I ask, Emily, and I will let you have a shield for that eye.'

He came back with it presently and adjusted it for her, but she didn't look at his face, keeping her gaze on his dark silk tie, and no higher. She was taken by surprise when he asked, 'How old are you, Emily?'

'Twenty-three, but I think you know that already.'

'You don't look a day over fifteen.'

He had gone, and she sat back mulling over the fact that while it was quite in order for him to ask her how old she was, it wouldn't have done at all if she had asked him the same question.

She got up presently after one of the maids had brought her a breakfast tray, and discovered that the headache hadn't quite gone and that her eye was more painful than she had at first supposed, but she had told Mr van Tecqx she was perfectly all right and she had no intention of giving him the chance to say, 'I told you so.' Not that he would, she reflected as she dressed. She sat down at the dressing-table and studied her reflection; the eye-shield gave it a certain cachet, she considered as she brushed her hair into a French pleat. It was a pity, she told herself, looking at the one-eyed face staring back at her, that Mr van Tecqx had changed, at least for most of the time. He had been warmly friendly when they had first met, and she had been drawn to him at once, but nowadays he had become cool, even downright cold in his manner, as though he didn't like her in his house, and the vexing thing was that, even in his most austere moments, she still loved him more than anything or anyone in the world.

It didn't bear thinking about. She powdered her nose and went along to Lucillia's room.

That young lady was sitting up in bed, reading her letters, but she put them down as Emily went in. 'Emily, whatever has happened to your eye? Shouldn't you be in bed? How mean of Sebastian to let you get up!'

'I wanted to, and it's only a black eye, the rest of me is quite all right.'

'You gave us all a fearful fright. Wasn't it lucky that Sebastian got home just as you screamed for help? He came to see me before he left this morning, and I am to see that you do as little as possible.' Lucillia smiled widely. 'Dirk is coming for the day—he sent me those flowers over there. Sebastian says you are to have a rest after lunch.'

'That's as maybe, but not before I've settled you for your rest in the drawing-room. Shall we get started so that you're ready for Dirk when he gets here?'

With Anneke's help, the morning chores went smoothly. Lucillia even did her exercises under Juffrouw Smit's eagle eye without a single grumble. Young love, thought Emily, feeling at least middle-aged, could perform miracles.

Young Dr ter Beule carried Lucillia tenderly down to the drawing-room and Emily settled her in one of the high-backed armchairs by the fire. It was a bright morning and frosty, so that the snow still lay thick and white in the garden, and Dirk, going to look out of the window, remarked gleefully that if the weather continued cold they would be able to skate.

A silence greeted this remark and he turned to see two reproachful faces staring at him. He was a resourceful young man; he went on without a noticeable pause, 'We'll wrap you up in furs and woolly things, Lucillia, and put you into a chair with runners and I'll whizz you round. There must be one in your attic?'

She was smiling again. 'Oh, yes, there is—we'll all go. Emily, can you skate?'

'No, but I'd love to come and watch.'

'But you must skate—we'll get Sebastian to teach you.'

Emily was saved from replying by the appearance of the coffee tray brought in by Bas, with a message from Anneke to say that she had made the little biscuits Dr ter Beule had enjoyed, and when they had had their coffee she excused herself with the plea that she had things to see to in Lucillia's room. Not that either of her companions listened; they smiled vaguely at her as she went and became at once engrossed in each other.

Emily was tidying away the magazines and books strewn around Lucillia's room when Bas came to tell her that Mevrouw van Tecqx had arrived and wished to see her.

She was in the small sitting-room, and rather to Emily's surprise had not as yet seen Lucillia. 'I came to see you, my dear, and since Sebastian tells me that young Dirk ter Beule is spending the day with Lucillia, I will look in on them only briefly. Bas is being kind and bringing me some coffee—will you have another cup with me? Do sit down. Your poor eye, it must be giving you a good deal of pain? Sebastian tells me there is no damage done, for which we must be thankful, but I could wish that you had stayed in bed and rested.'

She paused while Bas arranged the coffee tray on a table at her elbow, and when she had poured them each a cup said, 'Sebastian was greatly upset. He telephoned me yesterday evening—it was a very brave thing to do, Emily.'

'But there was no need, and I've given everyone a lot of extra trouble and work. Mr van Tecqx was quite right when he called me a little fool.'

'Did he indeed? I hope you put him in his place.' Mevrouw van Tecqx uttered the words sternly; but she looked pleased and a little smug, but by the time Emily glanced up from her cup her face was composed into its normal pleasant expression.

'Well, no...' Emily blushed a little at the memory of her childish burst of tears, and her companion noted it with satisfaction, although all she said was, 'We are all so very relieved that you weren't severely injured. I understand the man was wanted by the police for other robberies. Now tell me, child, have you good news of your father?'

'Yes, thank you, *mevrouw*, he's making a splendid recovery—very soon now Mr van Tecqx says he'll operate on the other hip.'

'The nurse is entirely satisfactory?'

'Oh, yes, and Podge, my cat, is very happy living at home. He never went out—only to a little back yard twice a day—when he lived in London with me.'

'You will go back there, to London?'

'Yes, I shall have to, so I can finish my training. But I'll be able to live in the Nurses' Home. Podge will have to stay with my father, but I'm sure he'll like that.'

'You, Emily? You will be glad to go back to the hospital?'

Emily said, 'Yes,' a shade too quickly, and her companion's blue eyes, so like her son's, sparkled at her private thoughts. A very enlightening little chat, she reflected with satisfaction, and declared her intention of spending a few minutes with Lucillia. 'Come with me, child. I need to say a few words to her about our gifts for Christmas, and you can entertain Dirk while I do so.'

Which was why Emily was in the drawing-room when Bas came to tell them that Juffrouw van Telle had called.

Mevrouw van Tecqx frowned. 'Will you show her in, Bas, and bring more coffee.' A request even Emily could understand now. She was timid about speaking Dutch, but if she listened hard she was beginning to unravel short, easy remarks.

Their visitor swept in, a fashion-plate in furs and soft leather boots which Emily instantly coveted. She didn't see Emily at first but made a great business of greeting the other before sitting down close to Dirk; she hadn't met him before and it was obvious that she was bent on charming him. Luckily, or unluckily for Emily, she caught sight of Emily's face and gave a little shriek of laughter. Emily couldn't understand what she said, which was just as well, but she could see the mockery on the other girl's face and the look of indignation on Mevrouw van Tecqx's placid features. It was Lucillia who spoke, in English. 'Emily has been very brave, catching a thief who knocked her down and probably would have killed her, only Sebastian saved her.'

Which somehow made the whole escapade sound romantic and Emily a heroine and left Beatrix van Telle looking foolish. She smoothed away the incident with practiced ease, but the look she shot at Emily spoke volumes.

Emily blinked her one eye and said nothing at all.

Juffrouw van Telle didn't stay long, and soon after she left, Mevrouw van Tecqx went too, giving a warm invitation to Emily to visit her at some early date as she went.

The three of them lunched together, but not before Lucillia had gone on her crutches to the dining-room with Dirk in close attendance, very pleased with herself and in high spirits. After the meal, she had insisted on going back again before Emily made her comfortable in her armchair by the fire.

'Now you must go and rest,' declared Lucillia. 'Sebastian said so,' and Emily went, aware that they wanted to be on their own and relieved too, for her head was aching, due, she felt sure, to frustrated rage at Beatrix van Telle's rudeness. There was a soft woollen rug on the chest at the end of her bed, and she rolled herself thankfully into it after carefully folding back the coverlet, put her head on the pillows and fell instantly asleep.

She awoke to a twilight room, lighted by one bedside lamp. Mr van Tecqx had drawn up a little table close to her bed and arranged an easy chair beside it, in which he was sitting, and she peered at him for a few moments in disbelief.

'Oh, good,' he said cheerfully. 'I thought we might keep each other company and have tea together. It would be unkind to intrude upon the two young people downstairs.'

A remark calculated to make Emily feel twice her age. She sat up and reached for her eye-shade.

'No, don't put it on; there's no need, it won't be the first black eye I've seen, nor the last. Is it any less painful?'

She felt at a disadvantage, cocooned in the rug. 'Yes, thank you.'

'Good.' He got up and piled the pillows behind her, and scooped her up so that she was sitting up against them. It surprised her a little that he did it so expertly. He poured their tea too, and handed her a plate with *speculaas*, the special biscuits eaten around Christmas time.

'Tomorrow, unless it's wet, you should wrap up warmly and we will go for a walk in the town. I have to operate in Rotterdam in the morning and shall be back after lunch. Theo is coming over to see Lucillia in the afternoon, and a good brisk walk will do you good.' He gave her another cup of tea. 'You have sensible shoes? There is a good deal of frozen snow.'

All her shoes were sensible. She said rather stiffly, 'I have stout shoes, and I should enjoy a walk.' Then she forgot to be stiff. 'I'm so glad Lucillia is happy with Dirk—I mean, they just sort of...' She paused, seeking the right word.

'Fell in love at first sight,' finished Mr van Tecqx. 'I hoped they would.'

'You mean you arranged it—that they should meet?'

He smiled and looked smug and modest at the same time, and she suspected he was amused. 'My dear girl, one doesn't interfere with fate. I merely asked Dirk to come to tea.' He got up. 'Which reminds me—Lucillia has begged to stay downstairs for dinner; would you mind very much if you settle her for the night later than usual? I hope you will feel able to join us. After a hard day in theatre I do not feel that I can play gooseberry without support.'

He wandered to the door. 'I hear that Beatrix van Telle was rude to you—unwittingly, I am sure. You must forgive her.'

'Of course, Mr van Tecqx. I dare say I would have done the same thing in her place.'

'Now there you are entirely wrong, Emily.'

After he had gone, Emily got up and did her face and hair and changed into the navy blue needlecord dress, adjusted the eye-shield and went downstairs. There was no sign of Mr van Tecqx and although Lucillia and Dirk greeted her with pleasure she quickly felt superfluous. Murmuring that she would get Lucillia's room ready for her, she went back upstairs and pottered around, putting everything ready. Lucillia had had a long day and done a great deal, she would be tired, and the quicker she was got to bed the better. Emily had to admit that Dirk had been the incentive she had needed; she was making real progress. In a few months' time she would be walking with a stick, and even though she would have to continue with massage and exercises, she would be able to go back to her home and lead a normal life once more. That meant that before long Emily wouldn't be needed.

There was a tap on the door and Anneke put her head round it. 'Mijnheer wishes you in his study, miss.'

She held the door open and Emily went past her and down the staircase. Now what? she wondered. Her father? A change of treatment for Lucillia?

She knocked on the door and went in.

Mr van Tecqx was on the phone. He beckoned her forward and handed the receiver to her. 'Your father,' he told her. 'Have a chat while I have a word with Dirk.'

Everything was fine at home. 'I've never felt better,' her father declared. 'Mr van Tecqx will operate some time in January. Will you be back by then?'

Emily had to say that she had no idea. 'But it shouldn't be much after that, Father. Lucillia is improving so quickly, I shan't be needed for much longer.' She enquired after Mrs Philips and Podge and then rang off just as Mr van Tecqx returned.

'Everything all right? Shall we go to the drawing-room and have a drink before dinner?'

The evening was a success. Lucillia was animated and happy and the two men kept the talk to trivialities, and Emily blossomed under their gentle banter, but, mindful of her patient, once the meal was over, she organised Lucillia's return to her room, then took herself off to her room for five minutes so that Dirk could say goodnight, then she went back to be helpful and put a tired Lucillia to bed. Her brother came presently to make sure that everything was as it should be before bidding her goodnight. He wished Emily goodnight too, so that any faint idea she might have had about going down to the drawing-room again was squashed on the instant.

Not that she would have gone, she told herself stoutly, she still had the vestige of a headache and her eyes throbbed. She got ready for bed and was turning back the bedcovers when there was a tap on her door and Anneke came in, carrying a glass of hot milk and a spoon containing a pill.

'You are to take this, and I must watch you, miss. For the head and the eye.'

Emily did as she was told meekly enough. If she had refused no doubt the master of the house would have replaced his housekeeper and stood over her until she had swallowed it. She drank the milk under Anneke's motherly eye and laid her head on the pillow. Five minutes later she was asleep.

She felt quite well in the morning; her eye was sore, but her headache had disappeared. She went to the window and looked out on to the dark garden. There was still a good deal of snow lying around and she hoped there wouldn't be any more until they had had their walk.

Her hope was justified; the day was overcast and cold, but there was no more snow. The morning went well. Lucillia, buoyed up by the knowledge that Dirk would telephone her during the day, was amenable to any suggestion which Emily had to offer and astonished Juffrouw Smit by her exemplary behaviour during her hated exercise period. Emily got her downstairs, settled her in the drawing-room and presently shepherded her into the dining-room for their lunch, listening with every appearance of interest to her companion's happy chatter, a hotch-potch of Dirk, new clothes, Christmas, new clothes again, and then Dirk once more, while she thought lovingly of Mr van Tecqx and their forthcoming walk.

She tired not to look too often at the clock while Lucillia, with maddening slowness, finished her coffee. Help came in the form of Theo, with little Willem in his Moses basket, for Lucillia was eager to tell her sister about Dirk. Emily got her back into her chair, asked Bas to bring fresh coffee, admired the baby and then went without apparent haste to her room to study her face anxiously and get into the stout shoes.

It wouldn't do to appear too eager, and how was she to know if Mr van Tecqx had returned home or not? She went along to Lucillia's room, plucked up a gossamer shawl and went down to the drawing-room with it, intent on spying out the land.

He was there, the baby lying across his knee, laughing at something Theo had said, but he looked up as Emily went in.

'Ah, you're ready? Forgive me if I don't get up.' He watched her give the shawl to Lucillia. 'Run and get your things—we'll be off.'

Buttoning her coat, Emily wished with longing for a new one. The shoes might be stout, they were also without a vestige of fashion and the woolly cap, while practical, did nothing for her at all. Most dissatisfied with her appearance, she went down to the hall, and found him waiting, coated and gloved, the epitome of elegance.

His glance swept over her. 'You'll be warm enough? We'll go to the Markt first and then along to the Koornmarkt and Lange Geer; there are three especially beautiful houses to see and several more of interest on the Oude Delft, and we might visit the Stedelijk Museum; you can see the bullet holes on the staircase where Prince William was murdered.'

He opened the door wide and with no further ado swept her out into the street. It was to be a lecture tour, mentally uplifting, she had no doubt, but very lowering to a loving heart.

CHAPTER EIGHT

IT WAS very cold, but the bitter wind had died down. Mr van Tecqx took hold of Emily's arm and started off at a brisk pace, the dogs at his heels. He was silent, but she sensed that it was a companionable silence and there was no need to make small talk. They reached the Markt and turned past the Stadhuis into the Koornmarkt, where they came to a halt to admire two lovely gabled houses on either side of the street. Mr van Tecqx had a sound knowledge of his birthplace; he pointed out the differences between the gables and the Gothic façade of one of them and talked at some length about Dutch Renaissance architecture. With anyone else, Emily would probably have been bored, but as it was, she listened to every word, not taking in anything of what he was saying, just listening to his voice.

They walked on presently down Lange Geer, to inspect another well restored house, and thence over one of the little arched bridges which she so admired, to the Oude Delft. There were very old buildings here too, the arsenals from the seventeenth century, and close by the East India Company House, looking exactly as it had done when it was first built.

They were nearing the Oude Kerk again and Sint Agathaplein, and Emily wondered if her companion remembered their first walk in the moonlight. Apparently not; she took a quick peep at his face which showed it to be unconcerned.

He took her along the Schoutenvleugel to the Prinsenhof and ushered her inside, with a quiet word to the dogs to wait outside. There were no other people there, only the curator, whom Mr van Tecqx engaged in a brief conversation before setting off on a tour of the building.

It was very quiet as they went slowly from one room to the next—it was a museum, but it didn't seem like one. Mr van Tecqx was an excellent guide, saying just enough and giving her time to stand and stare, ready to answer her questions. They came at last to the stairs and the wall where the bullets from Balthasar Gerard's pistol, first killing Prince William of Orange, had buried themselves in the plaster.

'You have a proud history,' observed Emily softly. 'You must be very happy to live here.'

'Oh, yes, I am. My family have lived here since the seventeenth century, in the same house. My mother's house is old too, but it wasn't until Napoleon's time that the custom was formed of the eldest son taking over the house when his father died, and his widowed mother moving to the house my mother lives in now. A pleasant custom, leaving the son's bride to take up the reins, as it were, until such time as it is her turn to do likewise.'

He led the way outside to where the dogs were patiently waiting and she saw that the afternoon was already sinking into dusk. 'Lucillia . . .' she began.

'Dirk does not leave until seven o'clock. We are going to have tea with some old friends of mine, Constantia and Jereon van der Geissen—he is a GP. She is English; they met nine or ten years ago—she was a nurse, and I think you will like her.'

The house was at the other end of Oude Delft, a patrician house with a great deal of plasterwork on its flat front. Mr van Tecqx gave the old-fashioned doorbell an almighty tug, and the door was opened almost at once by a dignified man whom Mr van Tecqx addressed as Taunus.

Urged forward, Emily entered the house, smiling shyly at the man who wished her a dignified 'Good day' in English and added, 'I shall fetch *mevrouw*: you are expected, *mijnheer*.'

He led the way into a large, grand room, its grandness made cosy by a tabby cat curled up on one of the enormous sofas, a tangle of knitting cast down untidily on a table and a pile of books and magazines on a sofa table. Emily barely had the time to glance around her before the door was flung open and Constantia came in with a rush. She embraced Mr van Tecqx and caught hold of Emily's hand, her pretty face alight with laughter. 'So you are Emily? I've heard all about you, but I don't suppose Sebastian has even mentioned me?'

Emily found herself smiling back. 'Well, no—only a few minutes ago as we were on our way here.'

'They're all alike—men!' declared Constantia darkly. 'Jereon won't be long—he went to see a patient. Take off your coats, do. Sebastian, sit down and take a nap or something while I show Emily the children.'

'All healthy, I suppose?' he wanted to know as he took Emily's coat.

'Bursting with good health. You'll see them all presently, they'll be down for tea.' She caught Emily by the hand. 'They're in the nursery—little Jereon and Sebastian go to school, they're eight and six, and Regina's three.' She led the way upstairs. 'Do you like

Holland? Delft in particular?' She didn't wait for an answer. 'Is your eye very painful? Sebastian was very bothered about it...' Emily thought she was going to say more than that, but she didn't, and since they had reached the landing, she opened a door and they went into the nursery. The boys were fair-haired and blue-eyed with high-bridged noses. They greeted Emily in English and wanted to know about the eye-shield, and when she told them she had a black eye informed her that they were going to be doctors just like their papa.

'Not Regina,' they explained, 'she's a girl.'

A miniature of her mother, Regina was having her hair brushed by a comfortable body in a large white apron. The room, reflected Emily, the house too had an air of content and happiness; it would be heavenly to be married and living with a doting husband and delightful children in such a house...

Constantia got up from where she had been kneeling by an elderly black and white dog; it was small as well as old. 'Prince likes to stay here in the nursery. He's more than ten years old now—Jereon found him...'

They went back downstairs, the children with them, just in time to fling themselves at a big man with greying hair and blue eyes under heavy lids. He hugged them in turn and then bent to kiss his wife. 'Hello, darling. This will be Emily?' He smiled and shook hands with her. 'Sebastian's in the drawing room? Good. I'll be five minutes.'

They sat around in the lovely room, having their tea; old friends who managed to make Emily feel as though she had known them for a long time too. When they got up to go, Constantia urged her to come again. 'We're only a short walk away and I'm sure you get an hour or two off during the day. You're not going back to England yet?'

Conscious of Mr van Tecqx's eyes upon her, Emily said demurely that she didn't know.

Walking back beside him, the dogs prancing ahead, she observed, 'What a delightful afternoon, and such a happy family.'

'I was a medical student with Jeroen; they're devoted—nice children too.' His answer was so casual that she decided to say no more; perhaps he was reminded of his dead wife. They reached his house in silence and once indoors Emily thanked him again and, chilled by his careless nod, went to her room and presently downstairs to see how Lucillia fared.

Emily had expected to find her tired, and she was, but she was happy too. Dirk was proving to be the incentive she had needed to get her back to normal. Emily prayed that the bond between him and Lucillia would prove lasting; it seemed likely.

Now he added his voice to hers in order to persuade Lucillia to go to bed early and have her supper there. 'You might just as well,' he said coaxingly. 'I'm on duty at seven o'clock anyway.'

He carried her upstairs and wished her a prolonged goodnight, while Emily obligingly fussed around in the bathroom, and promised he would find time, however busy he was, to telephone her the next day.

When he had gone, Lucillia said, 'I've had a lovely day. I'm so happy, Emily.' And then, 'I forgot to ask you, did you have a nice walk with Sebastian?'

'Very, thank you. The museum, you know, and some of the old houses...'

Lucillia took a look at her in astonishment. 'Is that all? What did you talk about?'

'Oh, the history of Delft...' Emily was bending over an open drawer, getting out a nightie.

'But Sebastian...' began Lucillia, then stopped, her lovely eyes thoughtful. After a moment she went on, 'I'm glad it's almost Christmas; everyone comes here for Christmas Day. Sebastian has to go to the hospital in Leiden for an hour or two, though, but when he comes back we have a marvellous dinner and dance afterwards.'

Emily heard the hesitation. 'I should think if Dirk could come even for an hour or two, you might dance a few steps; I know you won't be able to do much, but he can hold you up, and if you were to wear a long, full skirt, who's to know?'

'Emily, how clever you are. I'll surprise everyone!'

'Of course you will. But you'll have to work at your exercises and walking—it's only a couple of weeks away, and you'll have to rest for part of the day. You must promise that.'

'I'll promise you anything, darling Emily. We won't tell anyone.'

'Not a soul!'

It made it easier, somehow, immersing herself in Lucillia's firm resolve to surprise everyone at Christmas. Emily saw practically nothing at all of Mr van Tecqx; he came and went, and when he was at home more often than not he was in his study. Twice a day he saw his sister, listened to Emily's reports on her and pronounced his satisfaction as to her progress, but he made no further suggestions that he and she might go sightseeing again. She wrapped up her presents and after a good deal of deliberation, bought a leather-framed desk calendar for him. It would look strange if she didn't give him a gift as well as everyone else, but on the other hand it had to be something suitable and impersonal. She wrote 'With best wishes, Emily' on the card and put it with the others.

Lucillia's sisters came and went, and so did her mother; they were a close-knit family and liked and respected. 'They've lived here for ever,' Constantia told her when they met one afternoon by chance. 'For all I know Sebastian's ancestor ate his dinners with William of Orange. There's been a Jonkheer van Tecqx in Delft since I don't know when.'

'Oh, is that an uncle or someone?'

'Didn't anyone tell you? No, they wouldn't; they're the most unboastful family I've ever met. Sebastian's the current Jonkheer. If and when he marries again his son will be Jonkheer after him. Jereon's a baron, but I had no idea of it until we'd been married quite a time.' She went a delightful pink. 'He and Sebastian are the sort of men who hide their light under a bushel. Do you like Sebastian?'

Emily examined the display in the the shop window by which they were standing. 'Oh, yes. He's been extremely kind to my father and me. I can never thank him enough for that.'

She tried to keep her voice cool and only succeeded in making it wooden, so that Constantia gave her a quick look. They parted presently and Constantia said, 'I'll give you a ring—you must come and see us again. I'll get Sebastian to come too so that we get a chance to talk.'

At home, with the children in bed, sitting in the drawing-room with Jereon on one of the vast sofas, she said, 'I believe that nice Emily is in love with Sebastian.'

Jereon gave her a loving look. 'Yes, darling, I thought that too.'

'Oh, did you, and does Sebastian think so too?'

'He is not a man to wear his heart upon his sleeve, and I wouldn't dream of asking him.'

'Oh, well, I suppose we'll have to wait and see.'

'Time will tell, my love.'

Christmas Eve was upon them. Emily shook out the navy needlecord and the grey wool and wondered which to wear. She had a horrid feeling that everyone would be exquisitely turned out. It simply would not do. She took advantage of Mevrouw van Tecqx's afternoon visit to her daughter, raided her pay-packet and sped to the town's shops. She couldn't afford a new dress, but the grey was simple and plainly cut and could be dressed up. She bought a deep rose-coloured chiffon scarf for the neck and matched it with a wide belt—not leather, that would have cost the earth, but it looked like leather. Grey velvet slippers she unearthed in a small rather shabby shop down a side street, and matching tights. She hurried back and tried everything on. The result was pleasing enough, and even if all the women were in party dresses at least she would look a bit festive too. They wouldn't expect her to compete with them anyway.

Her black eye was normal again. She had discarded the shade and the swelling had gone, leaving a faint tinting of blues and greens and purple which, she told herself, didn't show if she powered her face lavishly.

She got back into the blue needlecord and joined mother and daughter in the drawing-room just before the first of the family arrived, Theo and her husband and small son, and soon after them came Jessica and

Jan with the twins, and Reilike and Sieme with their three children. The house was suddenly alive with children's excited voices and the steady hum of family gossip.

Lucillia sat in her chair, mindful of Emily's advice to rest as much as possible so that she would be able to do full justice to her dancing the next day. Dirk had not been able to visit her for a day or two, but he had managed to get a few hours off on Christmas Day, and as for the master of the house, he had been called away early that morning and no one had seen him since.

He came in quietly just as they finished tea. He truly looked tired, but he made no objection when the children rushed at him, shouting and laughing.

He made the rounds of his guests, kissing his mother and sisters, shaking his brothers-in-law by the hand, and paused finally by Emily, sitting mouselike where she could keep an eye on Lucillia.

He said without preamble, 'There is a short service in the Nieuwe Kerk at midnight—will you come with me, Emily?'

She looked up at him, her grey eyes suddenly brilliant. 'Oh, yes, please!'

'Everyone else will go to morning church—you won't mind staying with Lucillia?'

It was like having a bucket of cold water flung at her. Of course, she should have thought of that; she had actually allowed herself to think that he wanted her company. It wasn't like that at all, it would be a convenient arrangement.

She looked down at her hands, lying tidily in her lap. 'No, of course not, Mr van Tecqx. I expected that.'

He nodded, and presently moved away to sit with his mother and drink the tea Bas had brought in for him.

Mevrouw van Tecqx went back to her own house presently, although she would join them again the next morning, and Emily took advantage of the small commotion this made to get Lucillia into the right frame of mind to go to her bed. Tomorrow would be a long and exciting day.

Her brother carried her upstairs after she had had a drink with them all. The children were already being put to bed. Theo had brought her nanny with her and they had all trooped upstairs happily enough, eager for the morning and their presents.

Emily did not hurry over putting her patient to bed. Mr van Tecqx's delightful family were all very kind to her, but all the same she felt shy with them and intended to wait until the last minute before going down to dinner. After the meal she could excuse herself on the grounds of reading to Lucillia or something similar.

So it wasn't until the gong sounded that she finally went downstairs, to find everyone crossing the hall to the dining-room and Mr van Tecqx waiting for her at the bottom of the staircase.

'Why did you not come down earlier?'

'Well, I didn't want to hurry Lucillia, she's tired and excited too. There's always some tidying up to do too, you know.' She looked at him and smiled. 'You've had a busy day?'

'Yes.'

He was standing on the stair below her so that she was almost level with him. He stared at her, his eyes very bright. 'But not too tired to take you to church, Emily.'

She tried to look away and couldn't. 'Is it a long service?'

'No, we shall be back before one o'clock.' He kissed her suddenly. 'Would you like to telephone your father after dinner?'

The kiss had destroyed her calm. 'Oh, may I? Then I would like that very much.'

He moved aside and she gained the hall, and they went into the dining-room together. There was barely a pause in the buzz of talk round the table, but Theo winked at Reilike sitting opposite her and smiled widely.

Hours later, getting into bed, Emily sleepily reviewed the evening. It had been, by the large, one to remember. Dinner had been a merry affair and she had been made to feel very much one of the family, even though in her heart she knew that wasn't the case. Just before midnight when the house was quiet, she had gone to the Nieuwe Kerk with Mr van Tecqx, and although she hadn't understood the service, she had at least felt that she had taken part in Christmas. They had walked home quickly, because it was cold, and indoors there was a thermos jug of coffee waiting for them.

Mr van Tecqx had had very little to say, but he had been friendly, although he had made no effort to detain her once she had drunk her coffee, so she had wished him goodnight and a happy Christmas and gone quickly upstairs; his own 'Happy Christmas, Emily' had been uttered in an abstracted manner as though he had forgotten that she was there. All the same she decided, it had been lovely being with him, even if the reason for her company had been one of convenience.

Lucillia was radiant when Emily went to her room before breakfast. Because the day would be long and eventful she had agreed to have her breakfast in bed and get up after everyone else had gone to church, but her family had thoughtfully called in as they went downstairs to breakfast to wish her a happy Christmas and give her their gifts.

She was surrounded by tissue paper, boxes and coloured ribbons, and demanded that Emily should inspect everything. 'And thank you for the lovely shawl, dear Emily—come here.' She put her arms around Emily and kissed her. 'Dear Emily, I am so happy, and I hope you are too.' She reached under the coverlet. 'And this is for you, from me.' When Emily hesitated she said, 'Go on, open it now.'

A little round fur hat; a soft, silky brown which perched charmingly on Emily's soft brown hair and turned the face beneath it to something approaching prettiness. 'Oh, it's absolutely heavenly!' she breathed. 'Thank you, Lucillia—I feel quite different in it.'

'You look quite different too. You're a *jolie laide*, Emily.' Lucillia opened another box and held up the contents. 'Look, this is nice, isn't it?'

Emily took off the hat and put it tenderly back into its box, then after a minute or two took it out again and put it on once more. 'Just to get used to it,' she explained as she began to clear a space on the bed for the breakfast tray which would be brought at any minute.

It was Mr van Tecqx who brought it. Emily, forgetting about the hat, turned to the door as he came in and went a bright pink at his, 'Oh, very fetching, Emily.' He put the tray down, kissed his sister and handed her a small, gaily wrapped box, which gave Emily time to remove the hat and smooth her hair into neatness while her pink cheeks resumed their normal colour.

'You go on down, Emily,' he advised her. 'I want to see what Lucillia has amassed for herself.'

She popped the hat back again and went away, her feelings mixed. It had been a marvellous present, but she was vexed that Mr van Tecqx should have arrived at the precise moment that she had tried it on. She must have looked a fool.

Breakfast was a movable feast, with members of the family coming and going as and when they were ready. The air rang with the compliments of the season as they drank their coffee and ate the hot rolls and toast. The presents, Emily was told, would be handed out just before lunch, which would be at midday so that the children could share it with their elders. In the meantime everyone would go to church. She had almost finished by the time Mr van Tecqx joined his guests and she excused herself as soon as she could. Presents or no presents, Lucillia still had her routine to follow. She did it reluctantly, grumbling a little, but, as Emily pointed out, she needed to be on top of her form for the rest of the day. Emily began to pick up wrapping paper and pile the presents tidily on the table before the window. The garden outside looked romantic, with a scattering of snow and the holly trees bright with berries against the far wall. To her loving eyes it began to be even more romantic, as Mr van Tecqx, with Sidney and Pepper at his heels, came round the corner of the house, making for the small door which gave on to the narrow alley at the back. He looked up as he passed and, seeing her, waved. She waved back and Lucillia said from her bed, 'That'll be Sebastian.'

'How do you know?'

'I can tell from the way the back of your head looked.' And when Emily spun round, very pink again, gave her a look of such innocence from her blue eyes that Emily told herself she was getting stupidly touchy. No one, she was confident, had any idea of her feelings towards the master of the house.

They had already in fact discussed what Lucillia should wear. Emily got the soft green crêpe dress from the closet and hung it ready. It had a long skirt, its pleats soft and ample, the small waist encircled by a supple leather belt with a lovely buckle. Encouraged by the sight of it, Lucillia did her exercises, had her shower and dressed laboriously with Emily giving her help where it was needed, taking no notice of her peevish impatience when her legs refused to do what she wished them to do.

At length she really was ready, and as though answering a cue, Mr van Tecqx knocked on the door, remarking as he entered that he had just returned from the hospital and come to carry his sister down. 'Tomorrow,' he told her, 'you are going to walk downstairs. I'll be with you and you can go step by step, sideways on, holding the banisters with both hands. But that is a treat for tomorrow.' He studied her, his handsome head on one side. 'Very pretty, my dear.' He glanced at Emily, smiling a little. 'Bring the crutches, will you, Emily?'

There was a magnificent tree standing in the corner of the drawing-room, decked with white and silver and lighted with white and silver electric candles. Round its base were the presents, four and five deep.

The three of them had their coffee, not waiting for the rest of the family to get back from church, and presently Mevrouw van Tecqx arrived, just ahead of her family. Emily slipped away presently; she would return in an hour, in time for drinks before the Christmas feast. She busied herself in Lucillia's room, tidying up, then went to her own room and sat down by the window. She wasn't unhappy, she told herself stoutly, only a little lonely, and really she was having a lovely Christmas...

Someone knocked on the door and she called, 'Come in.' The room had been tidied and the bed made hours ago. She supposed the staff were in their sitting-room until it was time to hand out the presents.

Mr van Tecqx came in without haste, and she stared at him in surprise, thinking at the same time, that he seemed to get larger each time she saw him. 'Lucillia——' she began.

'In the bosom of the family.' He came and stood by the window, towering over her. 'We have to have a talk, Emily. I shall operate on your father around the middle of January. I think that by then Lucillia will be, in every sense of the expression, on her feet, still walking with crutches, of course, but able to cope. Besides, there will be Dirk...' He smiled at the thought. 'They are very well suited and not too young to marry. They will have to wait for a few months, of course. I intend to marry first.' He watched the colour drain from her face with interest. 'You are surprised? I have, after all, only been waiting for a girl to come into my life whom I can love.'

'I hope you'll be very happy.' Emily's voice was rather squeaky.

'I have no doubt of that. Now, I think you might return to England when I go in January. You will wish to be near your father, and at the same time Lucillia can return home to my mother's house.'

Ready for the bride, reflected Emily unhappily, and said a shade too brightly, 'Of course, Mr van Tecqx, I'll stay at home until Father is able to cope with Mrs Owen and then go back to Pearson's.'

He made no answer, but after all, why should he? Her future really was no concern of his; other than operating on her father there was no further bargain to be fulfilled on his part. It had been agreed that she might continue her training at Pearson's—a secure job... Suddenly it held no attractions for her; living in this lovely old house, surrounded by comfort and Bas and Anneke's kindly attention, had given her a taste of what life could be like, although she would have been just as happy in a hovel if Sebastian had been there with her.

'You agree to my suggestions?' His voice broke into her unhappy thoughts.

'Yes, oh, yes, thank you. They—couldn't be better.'

'Good. Let us go downstairs; it is time to hand out the presents and the children are just longing to get at them.'

It took quite a time for him to distribute the packets and parcels; the children first, of course, shouting and shrieking with excitement, and then the grown-ups, opening theirs rather more soberly. Emily hadn't expected anything, nothing like the small pile of gaily wrapped gifts which were handed to her. Chocolates and scent and beautifully embroidered hankies, and in a long, beribboned box a fur scarf to match her cap. She gaped at it, her mouth a little open, and looked at the gift tag. From Mr van Tecqx, wishing her a happy Christmas and his best wishes for her future. He was watching her from his place by the tree, and when she looked across the room he smiled at her. He had never smiled quite like that before. Her heart giving a little skip and jump, she managed to look away with an effort; it was just Christmas and everyone got a little emotional. She thanked him presently in a quiet voice which betrayed nothing of her feelings.

He said, 'Tomorrow we will take the dogs for a walk and you shall wear it.' Emily nodded speechlessly.

The rest of the day was dreamlike. the sumptuous food, the shining glass and polished silver and the lights gleaming on the women's pretty dresses were all part of it, and later that evening after a buffet supper Lucillia was helped to her feet, and when someone put on a tape of a Viennese waltz, was whirled gently around by Dirk, who had joined them that evening. Of course, she didn't really dance, for he had held her close, supporting her, but it looked as though she did. Everyone came and clapped loudly, and when Dirk settled her in her chair again she was flushed and triumphant.

Her mother crossed the room to kiss her. 'The nicest Christmas present I could have wished for,' she declared. 'How clever of you to think of it, my dear.'

'I didn't, it was Emily.'

Which brought everyone over to Emily to tell her how clever she had been—all except Mr van Tecqx, who had sat down beside his sister and Dirk; their heads were so close together and they were laughing a little.

Getting Lucillia to bed had been an exhausting business, but finally she declared herself ready to go to sleep and Emily was free to go to her own room. There was the muted sound of music and laughter coming from the drawing-room, but she didn't go downstairs. She had murmured a general goodnight as she accompanied Lucillia upstairs, and with all the children safely tucked up hours ago, it left the van Tecqx family free to enjoy the remainder of the evening. She undressed slowly and when she was in her nightie tried on the hat and scarf once more. She had never had anything like them before and they would last for ever, reminding her of Delft—but only Delft, she reminded herself firmly; Mr van Tecqx had to be forgotten as quickly as possible now that he was going to be married.

She supposed his family knew the bride, although no one had said anything to her. It was, of course, no concern of hers.

She was up early and had had her breakfast before the first members of the family came down. Lucillia had wakened early too and wanted her tea, and once Emily had seen to that there was no point in her going back to bed.

It wasn't until mid-morning that Lucillia was ready to go downstairs, and Emily remembered that she was to walk with her brother's aid. She went downstairs and peered into the various room, looking for him, and found him in the library with the twins. He looked up as she went in.

'Hello—is Lucillia ready to come down?' He put down the book he was showing to the children. 'I'll come now.'

It was a slow awkward business, but achieved at last. 'Another milestone,' he assured his sister as Emily handed her the crutches so that she could cross the hall.

The pale blue of the winter sky was already dimming when he came into the drawing-room after lunch. Everyone was sitting around, gossiping idly or reading, and Emily was on the floor doing a jigsaw puzzle with the twins.

'Ready for that walk, Emily?' he asked and ten minutes later she found herself going through the front door, the hat and scarf arranged just so, the leather gloves Mevrouw van Tecqx had given her on her hands.

This time they walked to the Oostpoort, pausing to look at the Klaewshofje, one of Delft's very early seventeenth-century almshouses; the Oostpoort was even older, with twin pointed towers, but it was still lived in by two artists. There was a narrow swing bridge close by, but they didn't cross it but turned down Oost Einde beside the grey partly frozen water of the canal, and all this time they had almost nothing to say to each other. There was nothing unfriendly in her companion's silence; he had tucked her hand into his and his clasp was reassuringly firm, and somehow there seemed to be no need for words.

There were few people about and by the time they gained the house it was already dusk. At the door he turned to face her. 'I hope you enjoyed that as much as I have,' he observed.

Probably a good deal more, Emily thought, but only said, 'It was lovely. Delft is cosy as well as beautiful, isn't it? I'm glad I've lived here for a little while, I shall always remember it.'

She went past him into the hall and saw Bas with the tea tray going into the drawing-room. It gave her an excuse to go upstairs without lingering, which was a good thing, for heaven alone knew what she might have said if she had stayed there in the hall with Mr van Tecqx.

With Christmas over there was New Year to look forward to. The Dutch took only the two days of Christmas as holidays, although New Year's Day was a day when everything closed and families gathered to celebrate.

This time it was to Mevrouw van Tecqx's house that the whole family went, gathering on Old Year's Night in time for dinner and greeting the New Year with *olie bollen* and sherry or port and a good deal of kissing on everyone's part. Lucillia had been driven there by her brother and Emily had gone with them; as the clock struck midnight the champagne was poured and a toast drunk before the good wishes began. She thought happily that she had never been kissed so many times in her life before, and by the time Mr van Tecqx reached her, her cheeks were rosy and her eyes sparkling. He kissed her too, a gentle kiss on one cheek, and none of the other kisses mattered any more. All the same, she managed a calm, 'Happy New Year, Mr van Tecqx,' and added, 'But I'm sure it will be.'

In the grey light of the early morning she woke. In twelve days' time she would be going back to England; he had told her just before the party broke up and they had driven back with a sleepy Lucillia to his own home. He had expressed no regret, merely stated the fact in a quiet voice, and she had answered in like tones. Today he was going to Brussels for some consultation or other and then to Groningen to examine medical students. Time was running out; her dream world was at an end.

CHAPTER NINE

THE DAYS followed each other with unrelenting speed. Emily bought presents to take home with her and spent an afternoon at Constantia's home, sitting by the fire gossiping and playing with the children. Constantia had told her that she had intended asking Sebastian to bring her to dinner one evening, but she had been told he had too much work.

'Did you expect to go back so soon?' she asked, casually enough to make Emily answer impulsively,

'Well, no—I mean, I knew that Mr van Tecqx was going to operate on my father—I suppose I expected I'd stay here at least until father went home from the hospital.' She added hastily in case Constantia might think she was grumbling, 'I expect it's more convenient for him if I go back when he does. Besides, Lucillia has got so much better; that's because of Dirk ter Beule. They're in love, isn't that nice?'

Constantia, who knew all about Sebastian's quiet planning to bring about what seemed like a chance meeting between the two young people, agreed that it was very nice, and wasn't fate extraordinary sometimes?

Emily went to see Mevrouw van Tecqx too. She took a little posy of violets with her which her hostess received with cries of delight, despite the fact that, unbeknown to Emily, there was a large greenhouse in the grounds where an elderly and crotchety gardener cherished pots of them. She chatted about this and that over their coffee and remarked that Sebastian expected to be in England for some time. 'He has a dear little house, you know, in Knightsbridge—Montpellier Walk. Perhaps you know that part of London?'

'Well, not to say know,' said Emily, a truthful girl. 'I've walked around there on days off. It's a delightful part of London.'

'You lived near the hospital?'

Summer Lane with all its dreariness rose before her eyes—she had met Sebastian there for the very first time... 'Yes. But when Father is able to manage just with Mrs Owen from the village, I shall get a room in the Nurses' Home.'

Mevrouw wrinkled her nose. 'Is that not rather dull, Emily?'

'Yes, but it's convenient. There's hot water and lots of bathrooms and a laundry-room and games-room—a ping-pong table and television.'

Her hostess showed no enthusiasm for these delights. 'But you won't need to stay there for ever,' she pointed out hopefully.

Just at the moment Emily couldn't think of an alternative, but she said politely, 'Oh, I expect once I've qualified I'll try for a post outside London.'

She left soon after. She had taken a bus from Delft and walked from the main road along the narrow lane. The snow had gone, but the frozen ground was iron-hard, but she was driven back by Mevrouw van Tecqx's chauffeur, clutching a small packet that lady had given her as she was leaving. She sat beside the middle-aged chauffeur and wondered what was in it, and tried not to think that she wouldn't see Mevrouw van Tecqx again.

It was silly to get fond of people when you knew you would never see them again.

During the remaining days before she was to leave, Mr van Tecqx's sisters came to say goodbye, each of them observing that they would surely see her again. Emily, very much doubting that, murmured nothings and declared with unwavering enthusiasm that she was looking forward to going back to Pearson's, and failed to notice their knowing smiles.

Mr van Tecqx was apparently immersed in his work. He left early in the morning and returned in the evening to retire to his study or on several occasions, very correctly attired in a dinner jacket, went out for the evening. He visited Lucillia, of course, when he was coolly polite to Emily and scrupulous in his enquiries as to whether there was anything which he might do for her before they left.

'Your father will be in hospital, but I believe arrangements have been made for your Mrs Owen to stay at the cottage until you get there.'

'How did you know that?' asked Emily rather coldly.

'I had occasion to telephone your father about the arrangements for his transport.'

'Oh, well, he didn't say anything about that. I supposed Mrs Philips would be there.'

'She is taking a little time off, I believe, ready to take over again if necessary.'

'I shall be there.' Emily was a little peevish at his high-handed plans.

'Er—yes, but you might need to be away for some hours—interviews at Pearson's and so on.'

'I hadn't thought of that; I'm sorry.'

He had nodded and gone away, leaving her feeling vexed that she had been cross.

The last day came. Lucillia was inclined to be tearful, although now that she had Dirk she was prepared to do without Emily. 'But I hope we'll be friends for ever and ever,' she declared. 'You must come and see us; you get holidays, don't you? And Sebastian can bring you when he comes—he is always going to England.'

Emily agreed calmly and wondered what he would say to his sister's suggestion. For that matter, his wife might have something to say too.

Dirk came the last afternoon and Emily, with time on her hands, wandered around Delft, taking a last look at her favourite spots, especially the tower of the Oude Kerk. She would never forget that evening in the moonlight.

Back at the house she cast off her unhappy mood. There was nothing to be done about it; she would go back to hospital and finish her training and make a career for herself and, above all, forget Sebastian.

She was a little vague as to exactly where she was to go when they got to London; she supposed Mr van Tecqx would drop her off at the station so that she could catch a train home. That would be a good thing, since there was no chance to get sentimental in such mundane surroundings.

She set about getting Lucillia ready for bed just as though it wasn't the last evening, listening to her plans for the future—a rosy one with her Dirk—and discussed the desirability of a calf-length wide-skirted coat as pictured in *Vogue*. 'It could cover my legs,' reflected Lucillia.

'Also keep them warm,' said Emily, always practical. 'You'll have to use your gutter crutches for a bit, you know, and a long coat would almost hide them.' She added, 'It's a bit expensive.'

An understatement, if ever there was one. Lucillia shrugged. 'But Sebastian never minds; he has a great deal of money, you know.'

'What if you marry Dirk?'

Lucillia looked at her wide-eyed. 'Oh, he has a lot of money too.'

'Oh, well,' murmured Emily. She and Lucillia lived such different lives; she wondered what Lucillia would make of Summer Lane. Or for that matter, what Mr van Tecqx had made of it. What a pity she would never know.

They were to go by car, catching the night ferry from the Hoek of Holland. That way he could put in a day's work in theatre before leaving. Emily spent a trying day bolstering up Lucillia, who was suddenly aware that she would never be able to manage with Emily gone. She could dress herself by now, albeit slowly, and provided someone was at hand she could manage very well, and one of the housemaids had proved herself to be adept at giving the right sort of help. Juffrouw Smit would be coming each day to supervise her exercises. Mr van Tecqx arrived home in time to eat his dinner with Emily and, since it was the last night, Lucillia. There would be time enough to help her to bed before they left—besides, it would fill in the time very nicely.

With Lucillia in bed, her luggage waiting in the hall, Emily got into her coat, perched the fur hat on her head at a becoming angle and finally tied the scarf under her chin. She didn't pause as she left her room, because she might have burst into tears. Instead she went briskly down the staircase through the baize door at the back of the hall and wished Anneke, Bas and the housemaids goodbye. That done, she went back into the hall, because it was time to leave and Mr van Tecqx was a punctual man.

They all followed her. Bas put the luggage in the boot and the women came to stand at the door ready to wave.

Emily stitched a smile on her face and kept it there until they were out of sight of the house and driving through the darker streets of the suburbs, when she was able to look out of the window and wipe her eyes without being noticed.

'There are tissues in the glove box in front of you.' Mr van Tecqx's voice was gentle. Which made her want to weep the more, but she sniffed, blew her nose with resolution and sat quietly, staring ahead of her.

It was a short drive and the ferry was only half full; Emily made no objection when he suggested that she might like to go to her cabin at once, and once there, fortified by a tray of tea, thoughtfully ordered by him, she undressed, crying now as much as she wanted to since there was no one to see.

It was a rough crossing, but she had so much to think about she hardly noticed the heaving and tossing; indeed, she ate breakfast without demur, keeping her puffy eyelids lowered over her eyes. No amount of make-up could conceal her pink nose, but really it didn't matter any more what she looked like.

Her companion, watching her from the other side of the table, allowed his firm mouth to quiver slightly, but all he said was, 'It was a rough crossing—you don't feel too bad?'

She shook her head. 'No, thank you. About what time shall we get to London?'

He told her, and she sat wondering which train she would be able to catch. She would go straight home and unpack. Her father would have his operation the day after the next; that would give her time to get settled in, see Mrs Owen, make sure that Podge was all right and get some food in the house before she went up to London again so that she would be there during the operation.

Mr van Tecqx kept up a steady flow of small talk during the meal and she answered mechanically, relieved when they were bidden to get into their cars and go ashore.

It was a dark, grey morning, damp and chilly, but the car was warm and very comfortable and the road was almost empty. They made good time and too soon for Emily they were driving through the early morning traffic; Wanstead, Leytonstone, Shoreditch; the nearer they got to the city's heart the more congested was the traffic. Almost at the end of the Mile End Road she ventured, 'I can get a train from London Bridge; there are lots of buses from here...'

Mr van Tecqx said blandly: 'There is no need—dear me, did I forget to tell you that we are going to my place first? An early lunch, I thought, then I'll drive you down.'

It hadn't entered her head that he would do any such thing. 'There's no need, really there isn't. It's right out of your way.'

He had been driving steadily ahead and now he said, 'Well, we're almost there now. Besides, I thought you might like to see your father. We can call in at the hospital.'

'Oh, may I? You're very kind.'

He said thoughtfully, 'No, I'm fulfilling my side of the bargain; I haven't done that yet. You have, and now I must do the same.'

Emily fell silent at that and stayed that way as he took the car through the heart of London, along Piccadilly and so to Knightsbridge, where he turned off the main road into quiet streets lined with Regency houses, and presently stopped before a small house at the end of a quiet little street, bare trees lining its pavements, front doors gleaming with glossy paint and shining brass.

They got out of the car and Mr van Tecqx selected a key from the bunch he hauled from a pocket and opened the door. The hall was small, close-carpeted in red and delightfully warm. There were doors on either side and another by the small curving staircase. Through this door came a small thin woman, in a print apron with a cardigan on top, her hair screwed into a relentless bun. She had a sharp-nosed face and boot-button eyes that twinkled. Emily was put in mind of a thin Mrs Tiggywinkle, and had the feeling that at any moment a duster would be produced and the pair of them would be tidied neatly away.

'There you are, sir, and the young lady. Coffee's ready, and as nice a lunch as you could fancy when you want it. I'll have that coat, sir.'

Mr van Tecqx took off his own coat, helped Emily with hers and handed them to his housekeeper.

'Nice to see you again, Mrs Twig. This is Miss Grenfell—Emily, Mrs Twig, my housekeeper, and one of the world's treasures.'

Emily shook hands and Mrs Twig said happily, 'What a one you are, sir, but I do my best.'

He ushered Emily into a room overlooking the street at one end and at the other a small garden with a high wall round it. There were french windows leading to it and although it was so small it was a pattern of neatness.

The room was elegantly furnished but restful too. Emily sat down near the open fire and, bidden to do so, poured their coffee. Mr van Tecqx stretched his long legs before the blaze and smiled slowly when Emily asked, 'Do you live here as well? I mean, you've got a house in Delft...'

'Yes, I come here often enough to need a home—besides, the family use it when they come to London. You like it?'

'It's charming, and such a dear little garden too.'

Presently Mrs Twig came to the door. 'Shall I show Miss Grenfell where she can tidy herself? And when will you want your lunch, sir?'

'By all means, and we'll lunch in twenty minutes if that suits your cooking arrangements.'

Mrs Twig sniffed. 'You've never had to wait for a meal, sir, and you never will, not as long as I have the minding of you.'

She trotted ahead of Emily to the small landing above and opened a door. 'There's three bedrooms,' she volunteered. 'Two's got their own bathrooms, the other bathroom is down this little passage.'

The room was charming; pale pinks and blues and a very soft pearly grey. Emily, doing things to her face and hair, wondered who had furnished the house. She could hardly ask Mrs Twig and she hesitated to ask its owner; he had a nasty habit of ignoring questions he had no intention of answering.

She went downstairs presently and accepted a glass of sherry and talked nothings a little anxiously, not wishing to sit in silence. Once or twice she gained the impression that Mr van Tecqx was on the point of saying something and then changed his mind.

Mrs Twig was certainly the treasure he had called her. She served up a delicious lunch of chicken soup with hot rolls, grilled trout with pepper sauce and light-as-air castle puddings with black cherry sauce and thick cream. Emily might be unhappy, but she was hungry too, although she remembered to engage her host in small talk, leaping from one topic to the next in her desire to appear perfectly happy and at ease. Mr van Tecqx encouraged her in this, leading her on gently while thinking his own thoughts.

He took her to the hospital after lunch, where she found her father, sitting in a pleasant little room, watching television. He got up as they went in, his face alight with surprised pleasure. 'Emily, my dear child, what a treat to see you! And look at me—almost a new man, thanks to Sebastian. I can hardly wait until the day after tomorrow.'

She hugged him fiercely. 'Father, you look so well. I'll come up just to be here while you're in theatre...'

Her father nodded and shook hands with Mr van Tecqx, who said he wanted a word with the Theatre Sister and would be back presently. Alone, Emily asked, 'You are really better, Father? The hip is all right?'

'As near perfect as possible. What a splendid man he is. And you, my dear? You were happy in Holland? Your patient is almost well again, I hear. You must be very pleased. You'll be all right at home until I get back? Mrs Philips will be there, of course, as soon as I return, so you can go back and finish your training as soon as possible.' He studied her face. 'You're a little pale, Emily.'

'It was a very rough crossing,' she said, and that answer satisfied him.

Mr van Tecqx came back presently, and she said goodbye to her father and got into the Bentley and was driven back to the little house where Mrs Twig had tea and a luscious fruit cake waiting for them, and in less than an hour they were in the car again, driving down to Eynsford.

Dusk was gathering as Mr van Tecqx drew up before her home, and she was surprised to see there was a light in the sitting-room.

'I asked Mrs Owen to pop in,' he explained as he got out to open her door. 'She said she would stay until we got here.'

'That was awfully kind of you.' Emily threw him a grateful glance as the cottage door opened and Mrs Owen's comfortable figure was silhouetted against the light.

He gave Emily a little push. 'You go ahead, I'll bring your case.'

Emily flung her arms round Mrs Owen and then scooped up Podge, holding his plump, furry body close to her face. She felt like bursting into tears, although she wasn't sure why, but by the time Mr van Tecqx came in Mrs Owen was putting on her hat and coat, ready to go home, and in the ensuing bustle she pulled herself together.

'You'll not need me tomorrow,' said Mrs Owen, on the point of leaving. 'I'll be in the next day—leave the key under the mat, love, and I'll see to Podge. There's coffee and biscuits ready in the kitchen.'

'While you are taking off your coat I'll run Mrs Owen home,' said Mr van Tecqx, and to that lady's delight settled her in the car beside him and drove away before Emily had a chance to say a word.

Mrs Owen had done her best. The cottage was neat and tidy and there was a pile of washing to be ironed. There was food enough in the fridge too and clean sheets on the beds. Emily took off her outdoor things and turned up the gas under the coffee just as Mr van Tecqx came walking up the path again. He shut the door behind him and took off his coat, carried in the tray and sat down, apparently in no hurry to leave.

Half an hour, an hour perhaps, begged Emily silently. She would probably see him at the hospital, but never on their own like this. She put the thought from her because she must stay bright and cheerful until he went away. He must never guess.

She found plenty to talk about; Podge and Mrs Owen and their journey and how well Lucillia and Dirk were getting on and what a nice young man he was... He stopped her in full spate. 'You like the things I like, Emily; old buildings and quiet canals and animals and babies and small children.' His voice was suddenly harsh. 'My wife disliked children—animals too; she liked to dance and dine out and buy clothes. I was twenty-four when I married her—ten years ago. I thought I was in love; she was pretty and great fun to be with, and I imagined her living in my home, having babies, welcoming my friends. She left me within a year to live with an

American with a great deal of money. They were killed in a car accident a few months later.'

Emily sat like a small statue, watching his face. When he paused she said softly, 'I'm so sorry, Mr van Tecqx. You must have loved her...'

She smiled at him and he smiled a little. 'No, Emily, I was infatuated—that's something quite different. I haven't thought of her for many years now, but I wanted to tell you; I have been wanting to tell you for a long time.'

'You haven't wasted the years, have you? Think of all the patients whom you have helped and your family who love you, and you'll soon have a wife you'll love and who will love you too.' Emily looked down at Podge, sprawled on her lap. 'I'm sorry you've been unhappy, but that's all over, isn't it?'

He stood up. 'Yes, I think—I hope so. I must go.'

He was at the door when she asked a question which had been on the tip of her tongue for a long time now, and somehow it didn't matter if she asked it now. 'Is it Juffrouw van Telle?'

He looked at her blankly and then gave a great shout of laughter. 'No, Emily—there was never the remotest chance of that.' He started down the garden path. 'I shall see you after I have operated on your father.'

Emily watched the car slide away into the dark evening and closed the door firmly on its tail lights. There was plenty to keep her busy until bedtime, and when she was in her bed at last with Podge curled up on her feet she was too tired to weep.

She spent the next day putting the cottage to rights, doing a little shopping in the village and getting the ironing done. She hadn't expected to hear from Mr van

Tecqx, and she didn't. She went to bed early because she would have to be up soon after six o'clock. The operation was for ten o'clock and she wanted to be there, at the hospital, in good time.

They were kind when she presented herself at the reception desk. She wouldn't be allowed to see her father, but someone would take a message.

'If you'd just tell him I'm here,' said Emily, and went and sat in the waiting-room. The operation would take up a good deal of the morning, but she was prepared for that. She had a book with her which she pretended to read and after a little while someone brought her a tray of coffee. It was midday before Mr van Tecqx came striding in, still in his theatre kit, his mask dangling under his chin.

'Everything is fine,' he told her. 'They have just taken him to the recovery room. Go and have a meal somewhere—he should be conscious by two o'clock or thereabouts. You may see him then.' He nodded at her, unsmiling, and went away as quietly and as quickly as he had come.

It wasn't very far to the main street and some shops. Emily found a small café and had coffee and a roll and butter which she didn't want. The relief made her feel light-headed; her father would be able to get around just as he always had done, and even if he didn't work again, he would be able to go out and about, visit his friends, do his own shopping and, best of all, be free from pain. She found she was crying and, putting down her untouched roll, she paid her small bill and went back into the street. It was still too early to go back to the hospital; she wandered round killing time until a nearby clock struck two and she felt free to go back to the hospital.

Her father was conscious. 'Sebastian has just been to see how I am. He says everything was most satisfactory. He'll be in later on this evening. He's over at Pearson's now with a list as long as your arm.' He smiled. 'I'm sleepy.'

Emily bent to kiss him. 'And I'm going home. I'll be in tomorrow and I'll phone in the morning to see how you are.'

The cottage was dark and chilly. She fed Podge, lit a fire and turned on all the lights before getting herself some supper. She had just finished it when the telephone rang.

'I am sorry I had no time to see you, Emily.' Mr van Tecqx's deep voice sounded impersonal. 'Your father is asleep and the replacement was entirely satisfactory. He will be got up for a short time tomorrow. I may not see you when you come, but I will leave any messages with Sister. Goodnight.'

He had rung off before she could reply.

She got to the hospital just after eleven o'clock and found her father delighted to see her. 'But I still have to get up, my dear, rather a difficult business for the first time, but never mind that.'

He listened to her cheerful account of her day, admired the flowers she had brought with her and observed, 'Don't come tomorrow; there's no need. Sebastian tells me I should be out of here in two weeks or so. Mrs Philips will look after me then, so make your plans, my dear; I dare say Pearson's want a few weeks' notice before you can start again.'

'Yes, I'll write to them and make an appointment.'
Emily caught his hand. 'Oh, Father, isn't it marvellous?
I can't believe it!'

'Nor can I. I might still have been sitting in my wheelchair waiting for a bed. It's all thanks to you, child. You
don't regret it? I've delayed your training.'

'That doesn't matter, and I loved living in Delft;
everyone was so kind.'

'Sebastian told me you were exactly what was needed
for his sister.' He added, 'He has reason to be grateful
too.'

She saw he was tired, so she said goodbye, had a word
with the Sister, and went home.

Two days later she went again to the hospital, and this
time she saw Mr van Tecqx, but only very briefly while
he gave her a résumé of her father's progress. He had
just come out of theatre and was going back there again
for the afternoon session, so their conversation was
businesslike.

Her father was getting up each day now and the pain
was easing, so that walking was possible with the aid of
a crutch, soon to be discarded for a stout stick. There
was no need for Emily to go each day now; she would
telephone whenever she wanted to, he had books and
the television and was quite content to be there until he
was strong enough to go home. She promised to go again
in three days' time and went back once more to her lonely
home.

She had scrubbed and polished and washed and
ironed, and there was nothing left to do. She would write
to Pearson's and answer Lucillia's letter, but first she
would go up to London once more, not to the hospital
but to see Mrs Winter and take her the china windmill

and the Dutch chocolates she had brought back with
her. She caught an early afternoon train and took a bus
to Summer Lane. It had been raining and the wind had
blown fish and chip papers and sweet wrappers over the
street. Just for a moment she had a vivid mental picture
of the Oude Delft canal and the narrow brick street
running alongside it, quite quiet and clean and lovely.
She shook her thoughts away and started walking
towards her old digs. She had telephoned the hospital
that morning and told her father she would be going
there, and he had begged her to pay her visit in the early
afternoon. 'And give me a ring when you get home,
Emily. It's not a good neighbourhood.'

She had laughed, remembering the scores of times she
had gone up and down the street, and assured him that
her visit would have to be an early one since Mrs Winter
always went to the hairdresser's at three o'clock on a
Wednesday.

She had timed it neatly. It was almost half past two
as she thumped the rusty old door knocker and Mrs
Winter came to the door.

'Well, look 'o's 'ere!' she exclaimed. 'Back at the 'os-
pital, are yer, ducks?'

'Not yet, Mrs Winter. I'll stay at home until my father
is quite well—he's just had an operation.'

''as 'e now, poor old man? I've let yer room...'

'I'll be able to leave Podge at home when I begin work
again, Mrs Winter, so I can go into the Nurses' Home.
I brought you a souvenir from Holland.'

She waited while Mrs Winter opened her parcels, admired them and thanked her, and then she said goodbye,
mindful of that lady's hair appointment and her father's
wishes. The door banged shut behind her and she stood

for a moment looking up and down the street. It had begun to rain again and it was already growing dusk, which was why she hadn't seen Mr van Tecqx leaning against the lamp-post until she was through the gate.

He put out an arm and brought her to an astonished halt. 'We met here in the rain—do you remember? And now we meet again. Some people would call it romantic; I'd call it a combination of keeping tabs on your whereabouts and a hard-won patience.'

'How did you know I was here?' Emily was breathless.

'I asked your father to let me know if at any time you should mention where you were going. I had in mind picture galleries or museums or even one or other of the parks. I must say you choose your outings in dreary surroundings.'

'I had a present for my ex-landlady. Why are you here?'

He pulled her a little closer. 'We had a bargain; you fulfilled your part of it, I have now fulfilled mine. Which leaves us free of obligation towards each other. Do you know, my darling, the first time we met I fell in love with you? I wasn't aware of it then, it crept up on me unawares while I wondered why I couldn't get you out of my head. Now you are not only in my head, but in my heart too.' He put an arm around her and an old man going past said, 'That's right, guv, give 'er a kiss.'

'You could have said.' Emily was blissfully unaware of the old man, and even if she had heard him, she wouldn't have cared.

'Oh, no, not until we had done what we had promised each other we would do.' Sebastian sighed. 'Though I must admit I have found it very hard to keep my hands off you.' He had put the other arm round her now. It was a lovely feeling, warm and secure and comforting; she was unaware of the rain, only of his arms holding her close.

'You're going to be married——' began Emily, then laughed a little. 'Me?'

'Who else, my dearest girl?' His arms tightened, but gently. 'And soon. The moment your father can walk down the aisle and give you away to me.' He kissed her slowly and then again, several times. 'Say yes, my darling.'

'Yes, my darling,' said Emily, and after a moment she added, 'My darling Sebastian.' It sounded nice, she would have said it again, but Sebastian kissed her once more, standing there in the rain under the lamp-post.

The old man had turned round to look at them. 'Barmy!' he shouted, 'kissing in the rain!'

This time Emily heard him. 'It's very nice,' she said sedately, and lifted her happy face to Sebastian's tender look.

HARLEQUIN
Romance

Coming Next Month

#3025 ARAFURA PIRATE Victoria Gordon
Jinx had been warned about Race Morgan, skipper of the boat taking her
scientific research team to Australia's northern coast. But she's confident she
can handle it, as long as he keeps their relationship professional.

#3026 GAME PLAN Rosemary Hammond
Jake Donovan, so everyone says, has an infallible plan that makes the women
fall at his feet. However, when it doesn't work with reserved Claire Talbot, he
finds to his surprise that he can't forget her. . . .

#3027 SPELL OF THE MOUNTAINS Rosalie Henaghan
Sophie is determined to make a success of her motel—and has no intention of
selling out to the powerful, dynamic hotelier Jon Roberts. Her refusal only
sparks his determination, for Jon isn't used to women who say no!

#3028 JINXED Day Leclaire
Kit soon discovers that playing with toys all day can be a dangerous
occupation, especially when working for a man like Stephen "The Iceman"
St. Clair. The normally cold and stern owner of The Toy Company behaves
more like a volcano whenever Kit is around.

#3029 CONFLICT Margaret Mayo
Blythe's first priority after her father's death is to make the family business
pay—and especially to prevent it from falling into Coburn Daggart's hands.
Years ago, Coburn hurt her badly, and Blythe makes up her mind to pay
him back.

#3030 FOOLISH DECEIVER Sandra K. Rhoades
Allie has learned the hard way that men don't like intelligent women. So, on
vacation at an old girlfriend's, she conceals her genius IQ. Her scheme
backfires when Linc Summerville believes she is a dumb blonde and treats her
like a fool!

**Available in January wherever paperback books are sold, or through
Harlequin Reader Service:**

In the U.S.
901 Fuhrmann Blvd.
P.O. Box 1397
Buffalo, N.Y. 14240-1397

In Canada
P.O. Box 603
Fort Erie, Ontario
L2A 5X3

CHRISTMAS IS FOR KIDS

Spend this holiday season with nine very special children. Children whose wishes come true at the magical time of Christmas.

Read American Romance's CHRISTMAS IS FOR KIDS— heartwarming holiday stories in which children bring together four couples who fall in love. Meet:

Frank, Dorcas, Kathy, Candy and Nicky—They become friends at St. Christopher's orphanage, but they really want to be adopted and become part of a real family, in #321 *A Carol Christmas* by Muriel Jensen.

Patty—She's a ten-year-old certified genius, but she wants what every little girl wishes for: a daddy of her own, in #322 *Mrs. Scrooge* by Barbara Bretton.

Amy and Flash—Their mom is about to deliver their newest sibling any day, but Christmas just isn't the same now—not without their dad. More than anything they want their family reunited for Christmas, in #323 *Dear Santa* by Margaret St. George.

Spencer—Living with his dad and grandpa in an all-male household has its advantages, but Spence wants Santa to bring him a mommy to love, in #324 *The Best Gift of All* by Andrea Davidson.

These children will win your hearts as they entice—and matchmake—the adults into a true romance. This holiday, invite them—and the four couples they bring together—into your home.

Look for all four CHRISTMAS IS FOR KIDS books available now from Harlequin American Romance. And happy holidays!